. . . Frieda lay flat and rigid under the sheets.

"Where the hell does she get off asking you to wander around Oakland with a drug dealer and ask questions about another dealer who's turned up dead? My God, I just can't believe you'd even think of it!"

Frieda moved abruptly and propped herself on her elbow. One hand reached behind her to switch on a lamp, and Helen blinked in the sudden brightness. Frieda's face was flushed and stern. . . .

It was the same old argument. Helen felt drained of everything, every emotion, even anger. "I don't know what you're talking about."

Frieda shook her head. Helen watched her long hair swaying in the soft light of the lamp. "Oh, yes, you do, Helen. You always have to be tough, hard as nails, cold as ice, all the clichés. A big, bad dyke. It's been this way since day one, when you were with the police and now with this agency of yours."

At the mention of the agency Helen began to lose her temper. "I'm not trying to prove anything, Frieda," she said. . . .

But Frieda ignored her response. "You do it with me, too," she went on as she lay down again. "This detective stuff is taking you away from me, even worse than before. All you think about now is solving problems, solving people as if they were problems. What do I have to do, get involved in a crime before you notice me?"

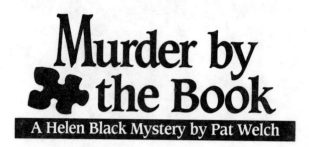

Murder by the Book

A Helen Black Mystery by Pat Welch

The Naiad Press, Inc.
1990

Printed in the United States of America
First Edition

Edited by Christine Cassidy
Cover design by Pat Tong and Bonnie Liss
    (Phoenix Graphics)
Typeset by Sandi Stancil

Library of Congress Cataloging-in-Publication Data

Welch, Pat, 1957—
    Murder by the book : a Helen Black Mystery / by Pat Welch.
        p.   cm.
    ISBN 0-941483-59-2
    I. Title.
PS3573.E4543M87   1990
813'.54--dc20   89-48971
                                                           CIP

About the Author

Pat Welch was born in 1957 in a U.S. Air Force base hospital in Japan. Upon returning to the states a couple of years later, her family lived in the rural South for many years before settling in Miami, Florida. After high school, Pat moved to Los Angeles, where she attended college and received a Bachelor's Degree in English. She later migrated up the coast of California to the San Francisco Bay area where she has lived and worked for four years. She currently resides with her lover and an assortment of pets. When she is not sitting in front of a typewriter, she can usually be found concocting something new in her kitchen or haunting the bookstores and cafes of Berkeley. *Murder by the Book* is her first novel.

*This book is dedicated
to Paula,
who made it all possible.*

Acknkowledgments

Many thanks to Barbara Grier, Katherine Forrest, and Christine Cassidy for their advice and encouragement.

Chapter 1

Bob unscrewed the cap of his thermos. The scent of coffee filtered up into the cold air and steam traced a delicate path that disappeared into the dark ceiling. The Berkeley branch of Greater East Bay Bank was completely dark except for the golden circle of light at the security guard's desk.

Bob Scanlon's fleshy hand took on a jaundiced sheen as he reached for the brown ceramic mug. "Kids," he muttered to himself as he sank back into the chair and sipped the brew. He wouldn't have had to be here at all tonight if that young pup Dwayne had showed up. It wasn't the first time Bob had been called on to fill in for him. Dwayne was probably out with his latest girlfriend at some party or other. Bob himself had promised Madge that they'd get the Christmas tree tonight. The grandkids were coming over, and they'd planned a little party of their own.

"I don't see why that supervisor always picks on you," Madge had grumbled while filling up the thermos a few hours ago. "Can't he get somebody else this time?"

It was the same old argument. "Now, Madge," he'd wheezed, zipping up the pants that seemed to get tighter and tighter, "he knows he can rely on me."

"Well, he needs to fire that kid then. What's his name, Dwight?"

"Dwayne," he corrected her. "Don't worry. Things will settle down after the holidays."

Remembering the conversation now, he realized that, truth to tell, he rather enjoyed being called on at the last minute. It made him feel responsible, knowing that others depended on him. It proved that there was life in the old boy yet.

As Bob sat there, feeling satisfied with his life and himself, the little travel alarm clock he'd set up on the desk began to beep at him, the sharp noise almost startling him into dropping his mug. Midnight — time to change the film in the security camera. He set the mug down reluctantly and plodded over to the closet to get out the ladder. Thank God Madge wasn't here to see him heave his bulk up on the ladder to reach the camera, nestled high above the manager's desk. Everything was fine as long as he didn't try to rush, dangling about six feet off the ground. Bob switched off the camera, opened the back and extracted the thick roll of film. Leaning against the wall he carefully placed the roll in the cardboard box that rested on top of the camera where he'd placed it last night. The replacement roll was ready, stuffed inside his jacket. Bob could also feel the thin flask of Jack Daniels pressing insistently against his fat thigh. Should he go ahead and take a little drink? It was pretty cold out tonight. Couldn't hurt, just for medicinal purposes. With a feeling of embarrassment stealing over him, he tugged out the container and took a quick pull at it. Warmth hit his throat and chest immediately, and he put the flask back in his hip pocket with a sigh.

It was then that he heard the noise outside. What the hell —? Jesus, it must be that tramp again. Maybe if he just ignored him the old guy would go away.

But this was different. Bob stood on the ladder, poised expectantly, listening hard. Several odd thumps succeeded each other, like someone was banging on the wall. Irritated at the interruption, Bob clambered awkwardly down the ladder, forgetting to turn the camera back on. The lens stared down at him, the red indicator light remained black. Bob had almost reached the back door before he remembered his pistol. He hesitated for a moment, then went back to get it.

"All right, old man," he called out as he unlocked the door. "What is it this time?" Feeling a little silly

3

holding the gun, like some damn TV cop, Bob stuck his head out, expecting to see the tramp cowering on the step.

But there was nothing. The fog, which had been getting heavier all night, lay like a wet blanket all around the building, filming Bob's bifocals with a soft mist. He hurriedly took off the glasses and wiped them with his handkerchief. It was the last movement he would ever make.

The blow came from the side, where a border of shrubs, now skeletal in winter desolation, hugged the back of the building. Bob's skull cracked under his cap and the big body sank like a boulder to the cement, sagging forward onto the steps. Another swift blow and it was over.

Voices pierced the air, sharp with tension. "You didn't have to kill him! My God, what the hell is wrong with you?"

"Shut the fuck up! What was I supposed to do with him, tie him up and leave him? There was no other way. Besides, he's just an old fart. Hey, what's this?" Slim hands encased in thin leather gloves located the hip flask.

"For Christ's sake! We've got to get him inside!"

"Will you calm down? There's nobody out here but us." The cap was screwed back on with a grating noise, the flask replaced in Bob's pocket. "Guess we better get him inside."

The body disappeared back into the bank by increments — first the bleeding head, then the huge belly, finally the feet, which flopped noisily against the door. "Holy shit, he weighs a ton."

"Come on, hurry!"

Finally the door was locked and all was silent

again, wrapped in thick white mist. The blood which had spurted out onto the cement was congealing quickly in the cold, leaving only a thin trace of death.

Chapter 2

The telephone was ringing as Helen struggled with her key. She was later than she'd intended this morning. Christmas shoppers were already taking to the streets of Berkeley on this last week before zero hour. Too late to stop the answering machine, she heard her own muffled voice addressing the anonymous caller. The "beep" sounded just as she managed to open the door, and the black lettering on the frosted glass glistened in the early morning light: "Helen Black, Private Investigator. State License #B774003-C9." When she had first had the lettering painted on, nearly six months ago, she'd felt a little bit silly. Maybe it was just a bit corny, as if she were trying to recreate a Dashiell Hammet fantasy. "Next thing you know," her lover had teased her, "you'll be keeping pint bottles in the locked desk drawer. Rye, maybe."

The door slammed open. At the same moment, the burden of books, newspapers and fast-food breakfast she'd been juggling spilled over her feet. The voice on the telephone went on, indifferent: "Hello, office of Helen Black. This is the garret of Frieda Lawrence. Just wanted to thank you for helping last night. I hope you'll make it to the exhibit tomorrow. Give me a call later, sweetie. Love you."

Helen bent, cursing, to the task of mopping coffee from the carpet before returning Frieda's call. Now she'd have to get some kind of cleaning fluid. The stain was too dark and obvious on the pale gray carpet. These days it seemed that all her petty cash was spent on such expensive but necessary items as were needed to keep up the appearance of running a successful detective agency. She'd deliberately chosen a new, attractive office building on Shattuck Avenue, just two blocks below the university. After weeks of worry and inner debate she decided it lent an air of prestige for the benefit of her clients.

Gathering up sodden paper towels, Helen tried not to think of the scarcity of those clients during the time since her name had appeared on the door. Six months of little more than curiosity seekers. Six months of seeing Aunt Josephine's small legacy seep away. Helen passed by her aunt's photograph in the silver frame, hung over her desk, on her way to the wastecan. Taken during the forties, the picture

7

showed a smiling woman with huge dark eyes laughing at the camera. For just a moment Helen saw her own dark eyes and heavy brows superimposed on the glass over her aunt's features. Helen remembered her as laughing at almost everything in her life, even at death. She could still hear her saying, as she lay in the hospital bed, "Don't you worry, Helen. I'll see that you're taken care of."

And so she had, leaving her enough money to finally quit the police force and get her license. Helen often wished her aunt could have been there the day she passed the examination. No one else from her family had made the journey from Mississippi to celebrate with her. They'd written her off long ago for the backslider and sinner she was. Still, Helen was sure that Aunt Josephine would have been very proud.

"Helen Black?"

Startled, Helen jumped and turned around. "Yes? Can I help you?"

The woman was large, in every sense of the word. Tall, heavy, big features, big hands — even her red hair was thick and full, streaming down over the broad shoulders. She wore a perfectly tailored gray suit, elegant in its understatement. No doubt it had been made especially for her. Her presence matched her looks. This was a woman who never escaped notice, and she was clearly accustomed to utilizing this to her advantage. Helen felt a moment of anger when she realized that the woman was well aware that even a private eye would be slightly intimidated by the aura of wealth and dominance, but pride soon took over. Helen stood holding the wastecan with as much dignity as she could muster.

"I saw your ad," the visitor said, coming a little closer. Helen took the newspaper she offered. It was a prominent Bay Area lesbian weekly. This meeting was the first response she'd had to the advertisement. "It says confidentiality guaranteed. Is that true?"

"Yes, it is, Ms. —"

The large woman eased herself into the more comfortable of the two chairs facing the desk. "My name is Donna Forsythe. I don't know if you've ever heard of me."

Helen reached into the top drawer for a pen and notepad, thinking that it would be hard for a lesbian living near San Francisco not to have heard of the Forsythe family. The paterfamilias, who bore the daunting name of Bailey Enders Forsythe, had amassed a huge fortune in the canning industry at the turn of the century. That fortune had steadily increased over the years, emerging unscathed from the earthquake and the depression. It was now largely invested in private and commercial property, a commodity always rare and expensive around the Bay. Although the family had struggled to keep Donna's name out of the papers, it was well-known in the gay community that she was in the habit of taking both male and female lovers. In the past few years, as AIDS had reared its menacing head, it was rumored that she was sampling the quiet life, settling down with one lover, a woman. They were supposedly living in a small cottage in Sausalito, north of the Golden Gate Bridge.

"Yes, I have heard of you, Ms. Forsythe. How can I help you?"

"If you've heard of me, then you'll understand why discretion is so important. I need help but I can't take the usual route. I —"

Here she stopped, and Helen sensed that admissions were going to be very difficult for her. Helen waited, fighting the impulse to fire questions at her, controlling her eagerness.

"It involves someone very dear to me. Someone who is in a lot of trouble."

"What kind of trouble?" Helen asked, pen poised above paper.

"Murder." Donna Forsythe laughed suddenly. "Sorry. It just sounds so melodramatic like that. Like something in the movies."

Helen smiled, hoping to put her at ease. "I know. It can be a little strange, coming to see a private investigator. Why don't you just talk about it? We can get it sorted out." She spoke in a soothing tone, trying to control the situation. Whatever she'd been expecting, it hadn't been this.

Donna Forsythe smiled wryly back at her. "I'm afraid it's going to take a little more than 'sorting out,'" she said. "It's my lover. Her name's Marita Spicer. She's very young, only twenty-three. I found her practically starving a couple of years ago, took her home with me, and generally took care of her. She left about two months ago and came back here to Berkeley. When I finally got her to talk to me, she told me she'd taken some job in a bank. I can't persuade her to come back, but at least she's letting me see her now."

Helen made a mental note of the possessiveness in

10

the woman's voice as she spoke of her lover. Her tone had hardened into near contempt when she mentioned the job at the bank. "You said it involved murder."

"That's right. It happened Friday. Or rather, Thursday night. The fifteenth. You didn't read about it in the papers? It was all over the place."

"No, I didn't." Helen felt a little embarrassed at her ignorance and had a fleeting memory of the last few lazy mornings in bed with Frieda. She looked down at her coffee-stained copy of the *San Francisco Chronicle*.

"Go ahead. Page one," Donna said, amused.

Helen read. It had taken place at the bank. The victims were Danny James, who was known as a small-time drug dealer, and Bob Scanlon, the night security guard. A search of James' apartment revealed that he'd also dabbled in pornography, using a photography studio as a cover. On the morning of Friday, December 16, the bodies had been found in the vault of a bank in Berkeley near the gentrified Elmwood district. The story disclosed that it was thought an employee of the bank must have been involved, although the police had no definite leads.

"Greater East Bay Bank," Helen read aloud. "That's over on College Avenue, isn't it? Just before Ashby." She remembered the small, neo-Victorian building nestled among old trees and restored shops.

"Yes. Marita started working there just after she ran away. I told her she was being silly, running off like that, but she was determined to do it." Helen watched as she shook her head, smiling as if at a wayward but lovable child.

"Do you have some reason to feel that Marita will

11

come under suspicion?" Helen asked, beginning to take some notes as she spoke.

The woman sighed and answered reluctantly. "I'm afraid so. You see, the police found a gun behind her desk. They've already been questioning her for most of the weekend. It wasn't until last night that she finally answered my calls, let me get in touch with my lawyer."

"Finding the gun behind her desk doesn't make her a killer, Ms. Forsythe. Is there anything else you know of that implicates her?"

But Donna Forsythe sat still and silent.

"If I'm going to help you, Ms. Forsythe, you need to tell me everything. I have to know."

Finally she replied, turning away slightly. "You're right. There is something else. It's her brother."

"Her brother?" Helen repeated, confused.

"Yes. Apparently he was mixed up in some drug charge a while ago. This Danny James was in on the deal. He got off, while Marita's brother went to prison."

"Where is he now?"

She shrugged. "He went into some halfway house in Oakland and got out of that about six months ago. Marita didn't say where he is now. I presume somewhere in the area. Maybe he's got a job of some kind."

It pained her to talk about him at all, Helen could see. In fact it was difficult to imagine someone like Donna Forsythe, cushioned by money from most of the thousand natural shocks that flesh is heir to, knowing people like Danny James, or Marita and her brother. She was probably already regretting that she'd even come here to talk to a private investigator.

"What exactly is it that you want me to do?" Helen asked.

"Marita's hiding something from me," the woman answered, blurting out the words in a rush. "I don't know what it is, but I'm afraid it might have something to do with all this — the murder, I mean."

"Do you think she did it?"

"What? Of course not! I mean, something from her past, something involving this James person and her brother. She's terrified right now, I can tell." Donna turned back to her, pleading with frightened eyes. "I'm sure the police are suspicious, too."

"So you want me to find out what Marita knows about this?"

"Well, yes, that's part of it."

"And the other part?"

The wry smile came back to the woman's lips. "I'm sort of a well-known figure around here. My family would be none too pleased if the name Forsythe were to be connected with an ugly crime like this one. Sooner or later the police will make the connection. If possible, I'd like you to find out who really did it."

"Before the police find out about you and Marita, you mean."

"Exactly. We understand each other perfectly."

Helen felt a sudden revulsion towards the woman sitting in the chair smiling at her knowingly. To hide her expression, Helen looked back down at her notes.

"I'll need to talk to Ms. Spicer as soon as possible. Does she know that you've been to see me today?"

"She does, and she's not too thrilled with it. Of

13

course, she thinks you're just a watchdog sent to guard over her. But I've told her you'll be coming to see her." As Donna spoke she scribbled on a sheet of paper she'd pulled out from her leather shoulder bag. "She'll be home this evening."

"All right." The address was further west, closer to the bay, in a block of newly built apartment buildings. "What time?"

"She gets off work at five. You'll have to call her."

The next few minutes were spent signing forms. As Helen watched her new client read them over, she wondered if she should go so far as to ask for a retainer of some kind. She'd never done so before — most of her clients had obviously had to struggle to find the means to afford a private investigator, but she knew that finding the money for this venture was the least of Donna Forsythe's worries.

"So I'm entitled to your full services until the case has been completed to your satisfaction," Donna read. "Meaning you won't take on other cases while you're working on this one?"

"That's right. The flat fee each day, plus an itemized list of other expenses that can be deferred until the final bill."

"I suppose a retainer is customary?" The woman smiled a little, as if she'd read Helen's mind and was enjoying her discomfort. "The contract doesn't say anything about it."

Helen had a flashback of her childhood — her mother dragging her by the hand through the Ben Franklin Five and Dime in Jackson, refusing to allow her to linger over the comic books and candy jars. "I said no and I meant it," she'd spat out through tight lips.

"But why not, Momma? Mr. Hadley always gives me a comic book when I ask for it."

Her mother's chin shot up, the lips became even more compressed. "Because the Black family is not beholden to anybody. That's why."

Feeling the blue eyes staring at her, Helen came back to the present. "Retainers are negotiable, as the contract states. However, given the serious nature of this case, I feel it should be part of our agreement."

Without a word Donna Forsythe took out a checkbook and scrawled on it. Helen forced her face into stillness as she read the generous figure. The woman saw through her nonchalance.

"You'll find I'm willing to pay for services. It's just wasting money that I can't stand." She slung her purse over her shoulder as she stood to go, and Helen followed her to the door, wishing she could appear unconcerned and blasé.

After she was gone, Helen went back to the window to watch her drive away. The dull bronze Jaguar was unmistakably Donna Forsythe's. It nosed its way through humbler vehicles like some magnificent fish in a sea of ordinary creatures and disappeared in the direction of University Avenue.

All the newspaper accounts of the murder told the same story, linking the deaths to drug dealers and calling for yet another crackdown on drug trafficking in the East Bay. Giving up, Helen reached for the phone and dialed a familiar number. In a moment her old partner, Manny Dominguez, was on the line.

"You're on the Danny James thing?" he asked excitedly. "How the hell —"

"Now, now, Manny! You know better than that."

"Oh, no," he groaned. "You're about to collect on a favor, aren't you?"

"I'm afraid so. Still in narcotics these days?"

"Yep. You make it sound like the latest fad."

"Couldn't you sort of stroll over to homicide and use your fatal charm?"

"Actually your timing is pretty good, Helen. We've had our eye on Danny James for a while, thinking he might lead us closer to that group of crack houses in Alameda. I guess I could use that one on Haskell."

"Not Haskell! He's in charge?" Helen winced, remembering Lieutenant David Haskell as arrogant and difficult. He'd earned a reputation for air-tight cases as well as for antagonizing others indiscriminately.

"You got it. Don't worry. I'll see what I can do."

"Great. Meet you at the diner at one?"

"See you then, Watson."

She hung up the phone, feeling a mixture of excitement and anxiety. If there was any information available, Manny could be trusted to get it. Helen couldn't repress a qualm or two. All her abilities, learned and instinctive, would be needed for this case. She glanced up to the portrait of Aunt Josephine, smiling down on her. "Wish me luck," Helen whispered.

16

Chapter 3

Manny was waiting for her when she walked in. The Alcatraz Diner had been one of their favorite lunch spots when they were partners. Its air of casual joviality blended well with an underlying elegance. Students and business people alike waited in line to be seated, and it was easy to pass unnoticed.

"How'd you escape from Frank?" she asked, referring to his current partner as she joined him in the booth.

"Told him I had to pick up a present for the little woman. He hates that kind of thing." He waved

17

to one of the waitresses, a slightly chubby young woman with curly golden hair, who immediately perked up and waved back. The girl deftly picked her way through the crowd to their table.

"I haven't seen you in here in a long time," she bubbled at him.

"Well, it's good to know I haven't been forgotten."

"Are you kidding?" she giggled. Helen rolled her eyes. Manny's movie star appearance had often won over reluctant witnesses, maybe even a jury or two. The effect of big shoulders, soft voice and velvet eyes was irresistible.

Once they'd ordered, Manny leaned forward and began tracing patterns on the tablecloth, speaking softly. "You've read the papers? The story is that it's an inside job."

"It's hard to see how it could have been anything else. What about the guard? Does it look like he was the accomplice?"

"Doesn't seem likely. He's been with the security company for twenty years. In fact, he was called in at the last minute to fill in for someone else, poor son of a bitch. He probably never knew what hit him."

"Was he shot?"

"Nope. He was hit a couple of times over the head with something, could have been a gun. The first hit did it, but our little friends made sure." Manny jerked his shoulders. "Pretty ugly way to die."

"What about Danny James?"

"He took one gunshot wound, at close range. Right in the chest." He tapped on his own immaculate shirt as he spoke. "James was found in the vault, the guard just inside the back door. It

18

appears the guard was knocked out on the back porch and dragged in. They would have had a rough time pulling him in much further. He was pretty big."

He paused as the waitress placed steaming cups of coffee before them. "Christ, it's as bad as ever," he said, grimacing as he tasted it.

"What about blood samples?" Helen asked.

"So far they all match up with the types of the victims. Hal said there was blood all over the place. It looks as though there was quite a fight in that vault — shelves knocked over, papers and files everywhere. They've set the time of death for both men at between midnight and one a.m. The film drop helped them with that, though."

"Film drop? What are you talking about?"

"Don't you know anything? It's all part of the security system. Every night at midnight the guard is supposed to change the film in the camera and put the roll that's been used in a pouch. Then it gets picked up by a courier the next morning, gets developed and stored away in some vault in Oakland somewhere."

"Let me guess — there was nothing on the film."

"Right again, Watson. The last thing on it is a close-up shot of that guard looking in the camera. When they opened up the bank next morning, the staff found two dead bodies and no film in the camera."

"What about prints?" Helen asked, but Manny was grinning at their waitress. He tore into his roast beef with gusto.

"Hey, remember me?"

"Oh, sorry." He swallowed and reached for his

19

french fries. "Nothing much to speak of, Hal said. Whoever it was knew enough to have gloves, like anyone who reads detective stories. They picked up a couple of what they hoped would turn into prints from the bloodstains on the floor of the vault, but it turned out to be from gloves. There were some shoe prints along with spatters, but they ended right at the vault door."

Helen thought hard, forgetting about the food in front of her. "So what happened to the shoes? They must have got taken off right there in the vault."

Manny nodded. "Shoes, coat, all of it. Everything would have been pretty badly stained with blood, since the gun used was a semi-automatic nine millimeter."

"Jesus," Helen breathed. "At close range? I'm surprised there was anything left of him."

"German made. There's a supplier used by most of the Oakland boys that specializes in German imports. The serial number has been partially obliterated with a corrosive, but the lab has restored enough of it to link it with a shipment stolen out of San Francisco last year. Our guys have been finding quite a few of these guns in Oakland."

"Kind of high class for a petty dealer, wouldn't you say?" Helen asked as she picked up her cold sandwich. "Danny James sounds more like the snub nose type to me."

"That's the whole thing about our Danny boy. He was small time trying to play with the big boys in Oakland. Always wanting to impress people. Even the police. That's how we thought he might lead us to the head of the crack ring."

"They're probably still testing the gun?" Helen

20

asked. Manny nodded, his mouth full. "There won't be any prints. Maybe some environmental traces, though."

"Yeah. The papers are not printing the fact that it was found stuffed behind a desk."

"But why put the gun there, rather than take it with him? Like the clothes and the shoes?" She was half hoping that Manny would say something regarding Marita Spicer that would indicate the attitude the police were taking toward her.

But Manny shrugged the question off. "Who knows? The whole thing is crazy. Two dead men and a wide-open vault."

"Managing the vault must have been the worst of it. They always look like fortresses."

"Hal was telling me that somebody screwed around with the timer inside, set it so that the vault would open up at midnight instead of the next morning at eight o'clock or whatever. Oh, he said there were some keys missing, too. They haven't turned up yet."

"Was there money stolen?"

"Sorry, kiddo. That's about where my information runs out. You're on your own with that one." He smiled, showing his famous white teeth. "It was at this point in my conversation with Hal that Haskell saw me." Manny upended the salt shaker over his french fries. "Did you want your pickle?"

Helen handed it over. "Great. I don't suppose you got to look at any photographs?"

"Are you kidding? The way Haskell operates, you'd never know the Berkeley Police Department had recently implemented a new policy of cooperation between all the major crime units. As soon as he saw

21

us in there talking, Haskell started grabbing files and grouching around."

"I hope you don't get into trouble, Manny."

"Nah! You know how it is — we all have to spray the territory once in a while. He'll get over it. Oh, I got this, too." He pulled a small sheet of paper from his jacket. It looked as though it had been torn from a memo pad. "I told Hal we'd need to talk to the staff of the bank about Danny James."

Helen read the names Manny had hurriedly copied:

Jerry Neely, AVP and manager
Lucille Ogden, operations officer
Ed Grant, chief auditor of the Alameda region
Lorie Harris, branch secretary
Evelyn Mayes, vault teller
Janet Strosser, teller
Marita Spicer, teller
Mattie Wilson, teller

"An auditor? Is there some kind of problem?"

"Apparently not. It's a regular thing. Once a year an auditor comes around and checks their records, watches their procedures, makes sure they're doing things by the book."

"Sounds like a pain in the ass."

"My money is on the Spicer girl," Manny said, spearing the last french fry on his plate. "I did some checking. Her brother got busted for dealing once before, in connection with James. But he's got a good alibi for Thursday night. He works out on the docks at Oakland and was helping unload a shipment all that night. Witnesses say he was there till dawn."

22

"What about everybody else?" she asked, gesturing with the list in her hand. "Where were all these people?"

"All tucked safely away in their beds by midnight, so they say. You weren't very hungry, were you?" He glanced down at her plate, still heaped with food, then back up at her, his eyes suddenly full of worry.

Helen ignored his question. "Could you do me a favor and keep bugging Hal about what was taken from the vault? There must be something missing."

Manny laughed. "You should hear him on the subject of the vault. Apparently the place was crawling the whole damn weekend with federal agents. I guess the FBI put Lieutenant Haskell in his place a few times. Hal said the old man was ready to shit bricks after trying to make those snotty agents jump through his hoops."

"I'm sorry I missed it." The waitress placed the bill face down on their table and Manny and Helen reached for it at the same time.

"No, no," he protested. "You did last time."

"You sure?"

"You'll just owe me a drink now." The crowd had thinned out, and Manny led the way to the cash register. Helen felt an abrupt surge of euphoria as they left the diner, walking out into warmth and the sun, unexpectedly breaking through the clouds. The wind, blowing in from the marina, was cold and damp. The sun would probably be hidden again in moments. Helen barely noticed the chill in the air. She'd suddenly realized that this case was her first big break — her first real chance to make a success of the agency. With a client like Donna Forsythe, anything could happen.

"I'm sorry, Manny. What were you saying?"

"I just said I hope you know what you're doing with this one, Helen." The light had changed, and they were crossing the street now, making their way to Helen's car.

"What do you mean?"

"Well, murder is a little different from finding kids who decided to run away from home."

Helen fought down a rush of anger that swept up into her throat and tried to turn it into dry humor. "Why, Manny! What a gentleman! Next thing I know you'll be looking for someone to marry me and take care of me."

Manny opened his mouth to respond, then apparently thought better of it. Although Helen rarely discussed her personal life with him, he'd been aware of her relationship with Frieda for some time. As partners, she and Manny had maintained a discreet silence on the subject of sexual preferences, choosing the better part of valor to keep things on an even keel with each other. The six months that had passed since Helen started the agency hadn't brought about any change in Manny's attitudes. He still backed away awkwardly whenever sex insinuated itself into a conversation.

Finally he said, "Come on, now, you know that's not what I'm saying. You can handle yourself all right. It's just that you aren't going to have an entire police force backing you up now. You won't be able to call in support if you need it."

Helen looked up at him. He was not being condescending. His face was quite serious.

"This is going to be an ugly one, Helen."

"Hey, don't get so worked up. Didn't I teach you everything you know?"

"Well — almost." He closed the car door for her, then leaned in through the window for one last comment. "Give me a call if you need anything."

"Actually, there is one thing you could do for me."

"Name it."

"Quit calling me Watson."

Chapter 4

Helen put her mug of coffee down on Marita's glass table. She'd been sitting in the young woman's apartment for over an hour, talking in circles around the subject of Danny James. They were getting nowhere. Marita clearly didn't want to talk. She stared back at Helen, her face a mask of boredom and arrogance. Physically, she was a sharp contrast to Donna — small and delicate, with black eyes and black hair that made her pale creamy skin seem even whiter. She wore silver earrings that dangled in huge loops from her small ears. Her attire was consciously unconventional in the standard Berkeley livery of shabby black layers from secondhand stores. Helen suspected her closet contained one wardrobe for the bank, another for "home." A double wardrobe — and a double life?

"I know you don't think very much of me."

Startled, Helen did not answer. The girl got up abruptly and started prowling around the room. She clutched her arms close to her body, hugging herself. Helen saw with a shock how thin she was, her legs sticking out from her skirt like rods.

"I must seem weak and immature to you. To go running right back to Donna like I did. A parasite, right?"

Helen noticed her white knuckles, the tension that made her voice break. "I wasn't thinking that at all, Marita." Somehow it had seemed natural to get into a first-name basis immediately. They'd been calling each other Helen and Marita from the beginning.

Marita finally stopped pacing. "Sorry. I guess I didn't know what else to do. After they called me in the second time yesterday, I got really scared. I let Donna talk me into this."

"By this I take it you mean me."

Marita sat down again and Helen saw under the light that she looked exhausted. "I'm not being very polite, am I? There are probably rules and a certain form to an interview with a private detective. Nothing like this has ever happened to me before, though."

"I understand. But I need to know a few things if I'm going to help you, Marita."

A hint of a smile played about the girl's lips. "You sure don't look very much like a private eye."

27

"One of my many disguises." They both smiled, a little shyly.

Marita sighed. "You want to know about Danny James? All right. I hated his guts. I'm glad he's dead. Okay?"

Helen waited. The rest came out quickly. "I left home when I was eighteen. My parents would have kicked me out anyway, since they'd just found out they had a pervert for a daughter. I decided to move in with my brother, Andre. Didn't Donna tell you any of this?"

"A little. I'd like to hear it from you, though."

Marita shrugged. "Anyway, Andre was living in Oakland, in the Rockridge section. He knew all about me, and he didn't care. We were both black sheep. Danny James was a friend of Andre's. Some friend."

"Did you know they were dealing?"

Marita shook her head vigorously. "I swear I didn't, not at first. I know it sounds naive, but it's true. I was just a kid. Andre said go to school, don't worry about working, get an education. He always seemed to have money, though."

"When did you find out about the drugs?"

"Well, one day Danny came over and he had all this stuff. I mean, he spreads it all out on the table like he was setting it for dinner, talking about all the money they're going to make." She smiled ruefully at the memory. "I never saw Andre like that before. I thought he was going to kill Danny."

"Why was he going to kill him?"

Marita looked at her in surprise. "Because Andre didn't want me to know anything about the drugs! Here I was, bouncing along, getting all signed up to go to the university, and then I found out that the

28

whole thing was financed by drugs. Andre had made Danny swear that he'd never stop by the apartment, never let me see or hear anything. All of it went down the tubes in one night. I sure got over being naive quick that night."

"So Andre was in on the dealing from the start?"

"Listen, you don't make rent in Rockridge unless you have some big bucks. I should have figured it out long ago. Anyway, I took off right away. Andre tried to get me to stay, but I didn't like the idea of getting killed in a drive-by shooting one night.

"Where did you go?"

"San Francisco. I tried to keep going to school, but it got too expensive. I met Donna in a bar where I was working one night."

"Did you ever see Danny James after you moved out?"

Marita looked uncomfortable with the question. "Look, Helen, Donna doesn't — well, are you going to tell her what we talked about tonight?"

Before Helen could come up with an answer, Marita sighed and shook her head. "Never mind. It'll be all over the papers soon enough."

"What will?"

"Danny's little sideline. His moonlighting." She looked up at Helen. "He was into other things besides drugs. He sold hard-core porn, too. Really sick stuff, some of it, a lot of S and M. He even bragged about using kids sometimes." She shuddered and got up to pace again. "He kept trying to get me to model for him, even wanted me to recruit other lesbians, if you can believe that."

Helen looked at Marita squarely. "How did he find you once you left Oakland?"

Marita hesitated just a second too long. "From Andre, of course. How else?"

"Did you ever do any modeling for him, Marita?"

"No, I swear it! Never! I hated him so much, I would have died first! But he wouldn't leave me alone. It didn't stop until I moved in with Donna. I was safe there." Her wide black eyes met Helen's, pleading and wet with unshed tears. Helen felt a vague uncertainty, a fleeting sense that the girl was acting.

"What about when you came back to Berkeley? Did you see him then?"

Marita laughed, a short sharp noise like a nervous cry. "Can you believe it, he came waltzing into the bank one day! I almost passed out. Of course, he didn't say anything to me then, he just wanted to let me know he was around. Then somehow he got my number and called me up. He said he wanted to take me out to dinner to talk about old times. Old times, Jesus! I figured I'd better do it, just to get him to leave me alone. I was afraid he'd keep dropping by the bank or something."

Helen decided to leave that piece of reasoning alone for a moment. "And did you go?" she asked.

"The day before he was killed. Thursday, the fifteenth. We met at the marina, at Figaro's."

Helen reached for her coffee again. "Tell me what happened. What did you talk about?"

Marita shook her head. "It was the same old shit. What a big man he was, how much everybody looked up to him. He liked to sound important. I shut most of it out and tried to think of how I could get out of there."

"Nothing at all, Marita? Take your time, think about it."

The girl frowned and considered. "Honestly, there was nothing. Unless you want to count how pissed off he got when I tried to leave."

"Tell me about it."

"Well, all through dinner I was just sitting there, not saying very much, when finally it all got to me. I mean, I was trying so hard to get away from shitheads like him and here he was messing up my life again. I remember telling him to shove it up his ass, or something like that. Then I got up to go, but he reached over and grabbed my arm and shoved me back down again. It hurt. He really scared me." Helen got the wet eyes again.

"What did he say?"

"Things like just because I went to college I didn't know everything. That when he made it big I would be sorry. It wasn't so much what he said, it was the way he said it. The other people were staring at us by then, so I just left, with him yelling after me."

"What do you suppose made him say all that just then? Why then, and not before?"

"Who knows? Unless he was planning on talking me into helping him with whatever was going to happen at the bank. But it didn't work."

Helen looked down at the notebook in front of her and sketched a few lines. "What did you do the rest of the evening?"

"Oh, yes, time to establish an alibi. Well, I went right out and had a couple of drinks."

"Where?" Helen still kept her eyes down, absorbed in her sketch.

"Where? Let's see. Geraldine's up on Telegraph. I had a couple of drinks there. Then I decided I'd better not make a night of it. Work in the morning. So I stopped by that women's coffeeshop further down Telegraph. That must have been around midnight. I can't think of the name."

"Mother Hubbard's?" Helen asked.

"Yeah, that's it! They closed just a few minutes after I got there, so I asked for a cup of coffee to go. I'm pretty sure they'll remember me."

"And after midnight?"

"I went straight home. I was pretty upset by the whole evening." Suddenly Marita got up. "Would you like something else to drink? Maybe some herbal tea?"

Although Helen detested herbal tea, she agreed. While Marita fussed in the kitchen, Helen got up to look out of the window. Frieda would like this place. For a studio apartment, it had a surprisingly airy feel. The high ceiling allowed for lots of light and space. The bay window in front of her was uncluttered — no shades, no cozy furniture. Helen could make out the university bell tower in the distance. A few lights were coming on near the campus, and fog was clouding the sky. It had turned much colder today.

"Nice view, isn't it? That's what sold me on this place."

Together Marita and Helen looked out over Berkeley. Helen wondered whether or not Donna had subsidized this rather upscale apartment. "It reminds me of my first apartment in Berkeley. Mine wasn't as nice as this, though." Helen did not add that when she'd first left Mississippi for California she had been

32

scared and hungry and lonely. She'd also been bruised
— her father had beaten her thoroughly upon finding
her with a girlfriend. At least she'd had Aunt
Josephine to take her in when she reached San
Francisco.

Helen turned away from the window and her
memories. "Is there some way you can get me into
the bank, Marita? I'd like to meet the other people
you work with."

"I don't know. That won't be too easy. Wait a
minute. There's that Chamber of Commerce thing
tomorrow night. Every month the Chamber of
Commerce holds this get-together for local businesses.
A different business hosts each month. It's the bank's
turn this time. No big deal, really — cookies and
punch and small talk. We almost cancelled because of
— well, because of what happened, but Mr. Neely felt
it would help morale to go ahead with it. We're
decorating the Christmas tree, too." Marita made a
face, rolling her eyes. "One big happy capitalist
family."

Helen laughed. "And it would be all right if I
showed up?"

"Oh, sure. I guess you'd qualify as local
business."

"True enough. What time does this take place?"

"Five thirty."

Helen gathered her notebook and her purse and
asked, "Where can I find your brother? I'd like to
talk to him, too."

Marita looked as if she was about to protest, then
changed her mind. "I'll write it down for you," she
said. Helen looked at the address and recognized the
area. It was one of the worst sections in Oakland,

frequently scanned by the media for its shootings and drug-related arrests. "I don't think he can tell you anything, though."

"From what you told me, he and Danny James were pretty close. The more I get to know the victim, the more I'll know about his killer."

"Victim," Marita repeated after her. "It's funny, I just can't make myself think of him as a victim. Not the kind of person he was."

"Even if you think he got what he deserved, Marita, there's something else you need to remember."

"What's that?"

"The fact that whoever killed Danny James is still out there, running scared right now."

Marita did not respond. She leaned against the doorjamb.

With the dim light from her apartment streaming behind her, Helen saw her in silhouette, the girl's face hidden in shadow. "I'll see you tomorrow night, Marita."

Chapter 5

Helen half hoped to see Frieda waiting for her when she got home, but the only greeting she received was a plaintive cry from Boobella, her cat. Looking like a baby panther, the cat leaped up onto the kitchen counter, which she knew was strictly off-limits, as Helen prepared her a late supper. "I don't know how you manage to eat this stuff," Helen sighed, stroking her thick black fur, feeling the rumble of purring. Boobella was the only link with home that Helen had kept through the years. The rest of her past she had tried very hard to discard along the way, although she knew that all she'd gotten rid of were externals. Her southern accent, her taste for heavy fried foods, even her tendency to take people at their word and drop over any time — all these things she could not pick up or put down at will. There were some things, though, that went much deeper than an accent.

Leaving Boobella to finish her meal, Helen called Frieda at her studio. Eight rings, ten rings; no answer. With mixed feelings of relief and guilt, she decided to organize the notes she'd taken that day. She spread the papers out on the kitchen table, deliberately avoiding going to her desk to work. Although the duplex seemed small and cozy when she first moved in, it now made her feel lonely. Her carefully collected furniture, most of it scavenged from secondhand stores and refinished, felt empty and useless, cluttering the space rather than filling it. Lately it was only when Frieda was there — laughing, arguing, gesturing wildly with her hands — that it felt like home. By herself, Helen gravitated to the kitchen and stayed there.

With a sigh, she tried to focus her mind on her notes. What Manny, her ex-partner, had told her had been clear enough, but she added a few comments of her own: "Check vault contents — anything missing? Who had access to timer? Film, security guard." She felt dismay as she wrote, realizing that it would not be easy to get any of this information.

Then she reached for her record of Marita's interview. Although they had talked a great deal about the bank and the staff, Helen was convinced that the girl hadn't been honest with her about Danny James. There had been the downward glance,

36

the wet eyes, the nervous laughs as she reiterated her alibi. She'd been lying about something. Helen flipped through her notes. Here it was: Geraldine's, a straight bar near the university, and Mother Hubbard's. That was the coffeehouse, a popular lesbian hangout. Helen put the notes away. It was more important to study what Marita had said about the operation of the vault door. Tomorrow night, at the Chamber of Commerce party, she would need to be prepared to see the right things, ask the right questions.

On a fresh sheet of paper she made three headings: Keys, Combinations, Timer. "It's a pretty set routine," Marita had said. The two officers — Mr. Neely and Lucille — have the combination to the dial, and two other people on the staff, Mattie and Evelyn, have the key to the lock and the key to the front door." The girl had drawn her a crude picture, showing the rectangular door to the vault, with a large dial in the center and an opening for a key just beneath the dial. "See? And the timer is on the inside of the door. You have to set that before you lock the door. They all take turns doing it every week. One week it's Lucille and Mattie, the next it's Mr. Neely and Evelyn."

"Who was on this week?"

"Mattie and Lucille. It was Evelyn's keys that were missing. Her set has the vault key and the front door key."

"When did she realize they were gone?"

"It was when we were all going home Thursday night. She was going through her purse for her car keys and said the others were gone. We all thought she'd probably left them at home."

37

"It sounds as though no one was too worried about it."

Marita had laughed. "You have to know Evelyn. She's the type who'd forget her head if it wasn't screwed on."

So she might have left the keys sitting around at the bank for anyone to find. Helen made a notation next to Evelyn's name and went to the next heading: Combination.

"I don't know how that could have been managed," Marita had said.

"It must be written down somewhere."

"It is, but I know they keep it in a sealed envelope in the vault. And the envelope is put away in a locked cabinet."

"Who has access to the cabinet?"

"Well, again, it takes two people with two keys. Mr. Neely and Lucille have one, and Janet and I have the other. The problem is, people are in and out of that cabinet all the time. We keep supplies of money orders and wire forms and blank checks in there, things like that. We get lectured every once in a while about making too many trips back there. Lucille tells us to plan ahead and get everything we want in one trip, not to keep calling her away from her desk to go into the vault."

Helen had tried to reconstruct Thursday's trips to the vault, but it was no use. Too many people, too many activities involving the vault. Then there was the timer. Marita drew another picture, showing a round dial with twenty-four hours marked on its face rather than the usual twelve. In the center of the face was a single hand, which would be moved to point to the number of hours the door was to remain closed. Any manipulation of the combination dial or the lock before those hours had elapsed would send a signal to the alarm company, which monitored the bank at all times.

"Who sets the timer?"

"The same two people who open up in the morning. It's Mattie and Lucille. Lucille sets the time and Mattie witnesses. Then they shut the door, Mattie turns her key in the lock, and Lucille spins the dial."

Helen went back to Manny's notes. He had said the time of death had been set at between midnight and one o'clock Friday morning, going by the time of the film change and by what the medical examiner had said about the condition of the two bodies. Rigor mortis had only just begun to set in, in the lower extremities. She had nothing as yet on the contents of the digestive tract, but it was probably not necessary.

So what would have happened with the timer? Helen shuffled back through her notes. There had been a visit that day from a service man from the alarm company. He'd been there to clean the door and its components.

"It's something that gets done twice a year," Marita explained.

"Who knew about it?"

"I guess we all did. Like I said, it's an ordinary thing. No big secret."

While making her sketch, Marita had described the timer as being very old. In fact, their branch was due for a remodeling, and possibly a new vault door, during the course of the coming year. "You can hardly see the numbers on the timer, it's worn away so much. They just look like notches now." Could someone have shifted the face of the clock while the mechanism was opened up for cleaning? It would have been an incredible risk. Why would anyone undertake to get the keys and combination, to handle the timer, when at any moment he or she might be observed? It was insane, a ridiculous picture: a shadowy figure, grabbing keys, noisily breaking open a locked cabinet, playing with a clock — all in plain sight. Suddenly an all-too-vivid image of what Danny James' body must have looked like, slumped on the floor in a slowly spreading pool of blood, flashed before her eyes like a scene from film noire, complete with trenchcoats and footsteps fading into the fog. Manny had said a nine-millimeter, at close range. She shuddered as she remembered what a gun like that could do. Only someone in great desperation, willing to take awful chances, would kill in this way.

The sound of Frieda's car pulling into the driveway made Helen jump. Perhaps she'd been a little unnerved at the thought of the corpse in the bank vault. Boobella, who for the last half hour had nested peacefully in her lap, wedged under the table, leaped onto the floor, disgruntled. Helen went to the door to greet Frieda.

"What on earth happened to you today? I called your office four or five times," Frieda said as she came inside.

They kissed briefly at the door. "Sorry, honey. I've been pretty busy today. I was out working on a case." Helen watched her take off her coat and hat. She shook her long hair down. The thick brown strands showed no sign of gray yet. The harsh light from the overhead lamp in the kitchen accentuated

Frieda's sharp, high cheekbones and long thin nose. She had on the red suede dress today. Helen loved to see her in it — Frieda looked so tall and slim in the dress. Helen always felt a little self-conscious of her own plain, rather square features when she saw her lover in this way.

"Rounding up lovers at the local bar?" Frieda joked as she went around the kitchen opening cupboards.

"No, not this time." Helen stayed near the door and watched her move around the kitchen. "This is the real thing. It's the first real challenge I've had."

Frieda located the brandy and a glass and poured herself a drink.

"Ah, that's better. What did you mean?"

Helen laughed sheepishly, aware that her answer would sound like something out of a B movie. "It's a murder."

"You've got to be kidding." Frieda stared, her face expressionless.

"Why?" Helen asked, nettled.

Frieda didn't answer right away. She reached down to pet the cat, holding her glass in her other hand, her eyes fixed on Helen. "I don't know why it surprises me. Maybe I just didn't want to believe it. Are you going to be in danger?"

"I doubt it. Our old friend Lieutenant Haskell is handling the case. He may be a pain in the ass, but he did always get results." She stopped when she got a look at Frieda's face. "Really, sweetheart, I don't think there's any danger to me. Don't look so — so stricken."

"Promise to be careful?"

"Scout's honor." Helen held up the requisite

41

fingers on her right hand in the pledge, and Frieda
managed a smile.

"It's that bank thing, isn't it?"

Helen was stunned. "Right. What made you think
of it?"

"I'm not sure. The timing, I guess." She got up
and went into the dark hallway, Boobella following
her.

"Frieda? What is it?"

As if letting go of something, releasing a force too
long repressed, Frieda stopped, then turned and
hugged Helen tightly, fiercely. "I don't think you
realize just how much I worry about you," she said,
muffling her voice in Helen's neck.

Helen felt the strange surge of fear mixed with
excitement, as she always did, at Frieda's abrupt,
spontaneous affection. She reached up to take hold of
her hands, trying to take hold of her own feelings at
the same time. It was a strained and wary minuet
they danced with one another, this constant pattern
of holding back and letting go, like a tide, with the
same irresistible drawing force. Had Frieda always
responded to love in this way? Or was it really, Helen
wondered guiltily, a mirror of her own behavior?
Frieda adapting herself, fitting her actions to those of
her lover's?

But as they kissed, Helen's own restraint was
overwhelmed, and she succumbed, almost reluctantly,
still afraid of the feeling of abandonment Frieda could
coax from her. She let herself be led to the bed, her
hand in Frieda's. Here all control was lost as they
took off each other's clothes, hurriedly, awkwardly, in
the dark. Hand on breast, tongue on thigh, face
buried in flesh — Helen felt her voice being torn

42

from her as she let Frieda take away the final resistance. It was always the same but never the same. Was it really boredom that drove lovers apart? Or was it fear? Helen forced all questions from her mind as they kissed again, lazy and sleepy now.

"Enough?" Frieda asked, a teasing smile on her lips as she let her hair play on Helen's stomach.

"You know damn well you wear me out."

"I like making you give up." She rested her head back on Helen's breast. Her voice was drowsy. "You're always a challenge."

"As long as I'm never dull."

"Never that." It was almost a whisper now, and Helen knew Frieda was drifting off into sleep. Helen continued to stroke her hair, her eyes fixed on the ceiling above. Not for the first time, Helen envied Frieda's ability to sleep, soundless and still, untroubled by thought. Suddenly, unbidden, Marita crept into her mind. Was she able to sleep tonight, dreaming sweet dreams?

Chapter 6

Lorie Harris woke early after a night of intermittent sleep. Her bedroom was close and stuffy, but her mother refused to turn the heat down. "If I did that, we'd all catch cold, and then just see where we'd be!" Sometimes Lorie wondered if her father had left them just to get some fresh air.

"Your oatmeal's gettin' cold! Hurry up!"

"Jesus, Mom. How many times do I have to tell you I hate oatmeal? Besides, I'm on a diet." Still warm and rosy from the shower and the blow-dryer, she poured herself a glass of grapefruit juice and gulped it down.

Her mother ignored her words and stared at her clothes. "Another new outfit? They give you another raise?"

"Yeah, right."

"You must be doin' real good, honey, for them to give you all them raises, unless —"

Lorie turned swiftly. "Unless what, Mother darling?"

"Unless you been doin' somethin' funny at the bank."

Lorie laughed, relieved. "Of course not, Mom! Actually I've been having an affair with Mr. Neely. He buys me presents, like clothes and jewelry."

"I know what you're like," Mrs. Harris muttered. "How you want fancy things all the time. I blame myself. I gave you everything you ever wanted, when you was little. You was always gettin' people to give you things, bein' all cute and smiley."

She turned away, still muttering to herself, leaving Lorie to stand alone in the kitchen. "Stupid old bitch," the girl said aloud to the empty room, trying to stem her uneasiness. Did she know? It didn't matter even if she did, Lorie decided. She couldn't stop her now. Humming to herself, she grabbed her new leather shoulder bag and walked to the BART station. Her leather pumps picked their way delicately along the alley, passing by the stacks of cans and bottles as she hurried for her train.

* * * * *

45

Lucille Ogden and her husband rarely spoke to each other anymore, now that the girls were gone. There was no reason to say anything. Over the weekend they'd talked about the murder, of course, but that subject had been exhausted. He stumbled into the kitchen Monday morning to get his cup of coffee and disappeared into the bathroom without a word.

She remained at the kitchen table, finishing the day's lunch schedule for the bank, trying not to think about Danny James. Would there be some kind of funeral? He'd talked about his family before, living somewhere around Sacramento. Perhaps they would be having some kind of service. Then again, maybe he'd lied about them, too.

Unbidden tears suddenly fell onto the large sheet of ruled paper she was writing on, smearing the ink. She wondered if anyone else would ever cry for him. She thought not. They didn't know him like she did. Memories of ten years ago flooded her mind and her body and she couldn't stop them. Not just now, not yet.

Lucille felt an odd sensation on her hands. Looking down, she saw a black, wet substance covering her palms and dripping from her fingers onto the table. Somehow she'd broken her pen as she sat there, thinking. Shaken, she hurried to the sink to try to wash off the stain, vaguely remembering something about Shakespeare.

* * * * *

"Here's your *Wall Street Journal*, dear." Jerry Neely's wife handed the paper over his plate full of

46

eggs and bacon. He speared more eggs onto his fork and continued talking.

"Not only that — we've got this goddam audit going on, too, with Ed Grant struttin' around like he owns the place. Reminds me of my old D.I. in the service."

"Now, now, Jerry, he's just doing his job."

"Hmph." He chewed for a few moments, looking over the batch of computer printouts piled high beside his plate. "He likes his job a damn sight too much for me. Like these daily reports of branch activity he's asking for now. He's just like those cops, following us all around with that damn clipboard, taking notes and sneaking around behind us." His voice trailed off into a grumble.

"Will you be home for dinner, dear?"

"No, not tonight. We've got that damn Chamber of Commerce thing going on."

"I thought you were going to cancel it." His wife spoke absently, a bland expression on her face. She clearly didn't care whether he was there or not. It was merely a matter of form to ask him.

"Well, I almost did, but I thought it would be good for everyone if we went ahead. You know, get things back to normal," he answered, rising and taking one last sip of coffee. He leaned over to kiss her and looked at her eyes staring dreamily into the distance. Sometimes he wondered if she really took in what he said anymore. Maybe it was just as well, lately. There were some things she just didn't need to know about.

* * * * *

47

"Oh, for God's sake, *shut up!* Quit complaining and just be glad you have a job to go to."

Janet Strosser turned away from her husband, stung. Of course he was under a lot of stress, being laid off again, but he never used to talk to her with such rage. Sighing, she went back to the tiny kitchen to make her lunch. Sandwich, apple, cookies — it was the same every day. Sometimes she just wanted to throw the whole thing out the window onto the sidewalk, sick of carrying the dull brown bag in one hand, like a school kid.

She heard Dave come up behind her. "Sorry, Jan. I didn't mean it."

"Forget it. I mouth off too much sometimes." They really couldn't go on like this much longer. She was too edgy, too drained, since the discovery of the body in the vault, to be very patient with him.

He tried to laugh. "Usually I love your stories about the bank and everybody there. It's just that this time — I'm really scared, Jan. I don't know what we're going to do."

"I know."

"The company may fold up entirely, Rick was telling me. Nobody else is hiring right now, either." He turned abruptly and left the kitchen, going to the sofa to throw himself down. Janet didn't follow him, knowing that he hated for her to see him so weak and emotional. "We may have to move back to your mother's if I don't find work soon."

"No!" At that she ran to him. "We can't do that!" Leave all this, the little condo they'd saved for and worked so hard to fix up? Leave the vegetable garden she started that summer in their postage-stamp back yard?

"I'm at the end of my rope, Jan," Dave moaned, tears in his eyes. "I don't want to do it either, but we might have to."

She returned to the kitchen, staring out the window over the sink. "No, we won't," she said firmly. "I'll think of something. Something."

* * * * *

Ed Grant was awakened that morning by the sound of his wife knocking over empty liquor bottles. He heard a distant muttered, "Oh, shit," then turned over to look at the alarm clock. Time to get up anyway.

"Sorry, honey," he heard Gladys mumble as she staggered to the bed. "Just wanted to get a lil' tomato juice. I've got this headache."

Why the hell did she keep up the pretense? Did she think it fooled him? Neither of them believed in it any longer. Once something might have been possible. He vividly remembered the last time they'd tried a support group. Pouring all the liquor down the sink, stocking the bar with fruit juices and soft drinks, hopeful dinners out to celebrate — then coming home after a week to find her passed out on the floor. He knew his private life was a topic of much gossip at the bank, but he no longer cared. His position as head auditor was impetus enough for them to stay quiet about it when he was around. No one wanted to antagonize him.

He looked in on his wife before he left, impulsively reaching down to stroke her hair. It was stiff, like a scrub brush. He never blamed her. He knew exactly what made her turn to drink for solace.

Time to go. He went to the hall closet to get his coat and grabbed his lined parka, the one he used to take on his hunting trips, a symbol of happier days. Even though he knew Gladys wouldn't wake up, he closed the door behind him softly.

* * * * *

All right, Mattie Wilson told herself. No use putting it off any longer. She reached for the thick envelope that had arrived yesterday from her sister in Miami, knowing that she might as well get it over with. At least her two roommates were gone, so she wouldn't have to show them the pictures.

She glanced over the letter, written in her sister's babyish script, with big round circles dotting the *i*'s. As usual, there were lines of wonderment at the Florida climate, at the swimming pool, at the sun, the sand, and everyone's respective tans. She looked at one photograph of her sister standing next to her third husband in front of their new white Cadillac. Nope, no resemblance. She, Mattie, was still short, dumpy and dark, while her sister had gotten the slim figure, the blonde hair, the big dazzling smile.

The oddest thing was that, more and more, Mattie was beginning to see a likeness between Lorie Harris, the secretary at the bank, and her sister. They both had that all-American prettiness that Mattie so desperately wanted. It was beginning to be a problem at work. Every time Lorie tossed her golden hair, laughed her most seductive laugh, or twitched a small gently rounded hip past a line of appreciative male customers, Mattie saw and heard her sister. If only the police knew about what Lorie had been doing these days!

Why don't you try to lose a little weight? You could use some make-up. If you act like that, you'll never get married.

The same lines that had haunted her from childhood sounded now in the empty apartment. She picked up the letter and the pictures and with a sense of brutal release, ripped them into small pieces, straining a little at the thick resistance of her sister's glossy image.

* * * * *

After Helen had left the apartment, Marita had slept well for the first time in days. She drove to work the following morning thinking calmly of the projects she needed to do — look up some records for Ed Grant, call up old Mrs. Hasselbach with information about her Social Security deposits, catch up on the bookkeeping. Routine had happily established itself once again, and Marita found herself humming to the song on her car radio. There had been no need, after all, to tell Helen about what she'd done that one time for Danny. It had been a couple of years ago, anyway. It wasn't relevant to his death.

But as soon as she walked into the building everything came flooding back. Bob used to give her a big smile on the mornings he was on duty at the guard's desk. They still hadn't sent in a replacement for him, and Bob's old coffee mug that had WE LOVE GRANDPA emblazoned on it was gone. The memory of the cold white body on the cement floor of the vault was almost a physical thing, like a clammy shawl settling across her shoulders, lying across her back. The mariner with his albatross, she thought, then fiercely pushed aside the implication of guilt hidden in the image.

"Hey, Marita! How you doin'?" Evelyn Mayes crooked her lopsided grin at Marita, the inevitable cigarette dangling from her full lips. Her nicotine-stained fingers riffled expertly through a stack of bills, and her eyes narrowed behind the bifocals as she inspected a bill closely. Janet Strosser, standing just to her right, looked up and offered her usual quick half-smile. Marita noticed that Janet's heavy makeup was already mussed, as if she had been picking at her face. She looked edgy again — maybe her husband hadn't found a job yet. Nobody liked to ask her about it because she'd usually just make some sarcastic remark or stinging rebuke.

"Any excitement?" Marita asked, plopping her purse down on her desk.

"Same old shit," Janet answered, biting a little more bright pink lipstick onto her teeth. "Lucille is on the warpath again."

"What is it this time?"

"Who knows? Maybe someone farted in front of her."

Evelyn giggled, puffing out smoke, and Janet walked away, secure in her sarcasm.

"At least one person around here is exactly the same as they were before everything happened," Lorie was saying. She strolled up to the counter languidly, brushing lint off of her jacket, then inspecting the rest of her suit with a critical eye.

"I'd be all right if I just didn't have to keep going into the vault," Evelyn said, reaching for another cigarette. "It gives me the creeps every time I go into that place." Her stack of money counted, Evelyn put the bills into a drawer, locked the drawer and left Lorie standing by the desk.

Marita sat down and began to open drawers, look for pens. She felt the other girl's blue eyes on her. "What about you, Marita?" Lorie asked. "Does it give you the creeps?"

"Well, sure. I mean, it bothers me just like it does everyone else." Marita never felt comfortable talking to Lorie. Aside from the fact that she always looked like she'd just stepped off the pages of *Vogue*, Lorie watched everyone too closely, storing nuggets of information against some future need. "It's going to take some time for us to get used to it."

"Maybe longer for some than for others."

Marita made herself look squarely at Lorie. "What do you mean?"

Lorie reached down and picked up a stray paper clip from the desk and began to fiddle with it, bending and twisting. "Well, I'd say you were pretty smart. I bet you can figure it out."

Panic rose in her, reaching up into her throat. "What on earth are you talking about, Lorie?" she asked, straining to keep her voice steady.

"Don't worry," Lorie sang out, tossing the mangled bit of metal back onto the desk. "I'm in the same boat you are."

She walked off, leaving Marita to stare after her. The fear came back, heavier and darker this time. What was going on?

Chapter 7

Helen found Andre Spicer's street easily. She had always hated this neighborhood — perhaps because it reminded her so much of her own back in Mississippi. This section of Oakland showed the same earmarks of poverty and apathy as her part of Jackson had: mediocre paint jobs peeling off onto the grimy pavement; wood showing the scars of termites, fire, or both; obscenities and political slogans splayed in block letters over every wall. That was one exception, she told herself — the graffiti she remembered was more concerned with racism and said nothing about politics or gangs.

Helen slowed down her car and began looking at numbers on the buildings. Here there were no trees, no plants of any kind, just rows of three-storied tenement buildings, flanked by useless cars left to rust away in the elements. A few homeless people huddled in the doorways and alleys, some openly rummaging through garbage, most waiting for a little warmth to filter down through the dissipating fog. Once she'd parked, Helen got out of her car slowly , turning a wary eye on the man crossing the street behind her. He looked harmless enough, cold and bedraggled like the rest of the people hanging around, but her years of experience had taught her that appearances could be deceptive on the street. The man disappeared into an alley, and Helen approached the building where Andre lived.

Two old women bundled in rags leaned against the wall by the curb where Helen parked her car, and they watched her silently as she went across the street to Andre's apartment building. She climbed stairs that reeked of urine and sweat, and though it was still early, she could already hear the thud of a radio playing rap music vibrating through the thin walls.

Andre Spicer might almost have been waiting for her, he answered the door so quickly. Marita must have called him last night. Helen's outstretched hand seemed to confuse him, and he shook it timidly. His palms were cold but sweaty.

"Marita told me you wanted to talk to me," he said, confirming her suspicions.

"Then you know why I'm here," Helen said,

moving closer into the room without waiting for him to do the polite thing and invite her in to sit down. He was small and delicate, like Marita, with the same fragile features, but the resemblance ended there. Where Marita's eyes had been dewy and youthful, her brother's were bleary, staring vapidly from under swollen lids. The left eye drooped a little lower than the right. Helen wondered if the strangely crooked stare was the result of some prison fight. He hadn't been toughened by his time behind bars — only beaten.

"Yeah, I know all about it." His voice was like his stare — tired and wary. He stood in front of her, his fists working around jerkily in his pants pockets. "You used to be a cop, huh?"

Oh, brother. "Yes, I did. I started my own detective agency when I left."

He sniggered. "Christ. Once a fuckin' cop, always a fuckin' cop. Want a beer or somethin'?"

"No, thank you." She sat down on one of the kitchen chairs at the rickety table and waited for him to return from the kitchen, beer can in hand.

"You know that Lieutenant Haskell?" he asked as he sat down. "What a prick." He took a deep swig, throwing his head back to swallow. "I already told him I wasn't there, so what the hell do you want to know?"

"Marita told me about what happened when she was living with you — how she found out about Danny James and the fact that the two of you were dealing."

"Hey, I ain't done none o' that shit since I got out." His small face was shining now under the yellow overhead light, his bravado crumbling fast. "I

57

don't need to go back in there, man. You know what they do to little guys like me? I spent my first three months in the hospital, they reamed my ass up so bad."

"No one is making you go back in there. I just want to talk about Danny James for a while."

He drained the can and began to rattle it on the table. The noise set Helen's teeth on edge, but she willed herself to stay still.

"You know he set me up?" Andre squinted at her.

"That's what I heard."

"Yeah, well, it's true. I figure he had it comin' to him, you know, 'cause he just talked too much. Like the last time I saw him."

"When was that?"

"Maybe a month ago. I just moved into this shithole apartment here, and then he shows up, struttin' up to my door, just like old times. I told him to go on the hell out of here and take that stuff with him —"

"What stuff, Andre? You guys snort up a couple of lines for old times' sake, is that it?"

"Listen, I told him I didn't need that shit around my place. But he laughed at me and said it was — what did he call it? A housewarming present. Yeah, that's it, a housewarming present." He cackled for a moment at the memory.

"Go on."

"Well, he said he had somethin' goin' on, somethin' big. I'm just smilin' and laughin' and not really saying anything, because like I said, he always talked like that. You know, tryin' to sound important. He won't tell me what it is though — just says it's the biggest thing he's ever done. So I go, what, you gonna round up some more junkies or what? Then he gets all pissed off for me laughin' at him."

"But he didn't tell you what this thing was?"

"No, not after that. He finally calms down and we finish the stuff —"

"Just to be polite, right?"

He looked at her, pausing for a moment. "Yeah, right. So I ask him if it's all right if I keep the pictures."

"Wait a minute. What pictures?"

"Shit," Andre muttered. "I didn't tell the cops about that one." He slammed the beer can down and walked over to a lopsided dresser. "I guess I can tell you, though, since Marita says you're okay." After rummaging for a while in the top drawer, he returned, carrying a large cream-colored envelope.

"He gave these to you?" Helen asked, taking the envelope from his hands.

"Yeah, he brought them over that night. Another housewarming present, he said. Told me he could introduce me to these broads if I helped him out."

Helen turned her face away from his heavy, beer-scented breath and took a stack of black-and-white photographs from the envelope. They were nothing unusual: several shots featuring ropes and chains and leather; a few showed hoods, dogs, and a variety of sexual toys. It was a depressing portrayal of sordid, desperate desire. The facial expressions of the young women showed nothing more than boredom, sometimes a twinge of fear. There was one, however, that stood out from the rest. This girl was dressed like the others, in black lace underthings and spiked heels, but her face had a true erotic beauty that set her apart from the rest of the models.

59

Helen would have said that she seemed to be enjoying herself.

"I noticed that one, too," Andre was saying, leaning uncomfortably close. "Wouldn't mind meeting her."

"Did Danny say anything about this girl?" Helen asked, not quite sure why she felt curious. Perhaps she was just unnerved at such beauty being revealed in this way, in spite of all her years on the force.

"Nope. He just kept going on and on about his big break."

They continued talking for a little longer, but he had no more useful information to offer. Helen rose to go, handing back the envelope.

"Here's my card. Will you call me if you remember anything else?"

"Sure, sure. Hey, lady?"

"Yes?" She turned to face him, her hand on the doorknob.

"Is Marita — I mean, is she gonna be okay? I don't want nothin' to happen to her. She's a good kid."

Helen looked at him standing there, one hand clutching the envelope, the other grasping the back of the chair she'd been sitting in. He looked like a nightmarish version of his sister, with the early morning light streaming in behind him.

"You know, I wouldn't have even given you the time of day if Marita hadn't called me," he went on. "I don't do jack shit for cops or private eyes, neither. But I think she trusts you."

"I'll do my best. Don't lose my card."

Chapter 8

Helen emerged from the antiquated phone booth at Mother Hubbard's Cafe and made her way to the lunch counter. Frieda had been a little disappointed at the news that Helen could only stop by the exhibit at the Women's Center for a few minutes that afternoon. "It's this case, right?" she'd asked.

"Right. I have a few things to do this afternoon. Sorry." Helen deliberately kept her answers laconic, not wanting to prolong the conversation into an argument. It was the same old story as when she'd been with the police — late hours, last-minute phone calls, and a hurt and disappointed lover.

There was a long silence on the other end, and Helen could hear the murmur of other voices. "All right," Frieda sighed. "I'll see you in a few minutes, then."

Helen ruminated into her cup of coffee while waiting for a chance to talk to Esther Howard, the owner of Mother Hubbard's. Right now Esther was explaining the use of the espresso machine to a new waitress, a pale blonde girl with a bewildered expression. Esther had presided over the cafe with fierce pride ever since she'd acquired it in the late fifties, when it had been a sedate tea shop for little old ladies. The formica and chrome trappings hadn't changed for a generation. In the strange cycles of fads and fashions, the decor was in style once again, a reflection of the current nostalgia craze.

Esther had finished her instructions and was back in front of Helen. "Poor thing," she muttered, jerking her head back at the girl struggling with the machine. "I shouldn't even have given her this job, but I think she really needed it."

"You and your strays," Helen chuckled. Esther was as much an institution as her cafe. She'd come to San Francisco on a tour of duty with the army after making a dramatic decision to leave her small Midwestern home town. Like many others posted on the West Coast, she'd fallen in love with the area and never left it. Most people, seeing her stocky build and gruff manner, preferred to admire her from afar, but Helen knew that the brusque manner hid an underlying sweetness and sensitivity. She trusted the older woman implicitly.

"So what was it you wanted to ask me about?" Esther came out from behind the counter and lowered herself onto the stool next to Helen's.

"I'm checking up on somebody. They said they were in here last week, on Thursday night."

"Well, I pretty much know all the regulars. Who was it?"

"This wasn't a regular. At least I don't think so. Very young, very pretty. She has short dark hair, dark eyes. Came in here just before you closed and got a cup of coffee to go."

"Thursday night, Thursday night." Esther threw her a quick glance. "That's the night of that murder over at the bank, isn't it?"

"Do you remember anybody like that?"

"She sat right here where I'm sitting now. I could tell she'd already had one or two too many. Really nice looking — you know I always notice those."

"Tell me everything you remember."

Esther shrugged and took off her glasses to polish them with her shirt. "There's not much to tell, really. The weekend nights are our big nights, you know, because of the live entertainment. I probably wouldn't have noticed her if we'd been more crowded. Me and Ellie were just getting ready to close up when she came in. She went straight for the counter and sat down, then she looked around and realized how we were about ready to leave. So she asked if she could just get a cup of coffee to go. I told her it was going to be like scraping the bottom of the barrel, the stuff was so old, but she said the stronger the better. Something like that." Esther replaced her glasses on her nose and looked at Helen with her usual impervious gaze. "Does that help?"

63

"How did she strike you, Esther? Scared? Upset?"

Esther scratched at her head, then said. "No. Not exactly. More — well, like she was thinking real real hard about something. Something was bothering her, but not upsetting her." Esther looked away again, assuming an air of indifference. "You gonna tell me what it's all about?"

Helen smiled and shook her head. "You know better than that, Esther."

"Right, right." The older woman got up and went back behind the counter. "Just make sure you remember me in your autobiography. Better yet, your will."

Helen finished her coffee and got up. Frieda would probably be along in just a few minutes. Helen sauntered over to the bulletin board and stared blindly at the notices — advertisements for rooms for rent, jobs available, seminars — but her thoughts were on Marita Spicer. Helen didn't even notice the other women who stopped to read the notices, some of them giving her appraising glances before moving on. Apparently Marita had told the truth about her activities the night the deaths took place — at least, up until just after midnight. But Mother Hubbard's cafe was not so very far from College Avenue, where the bank was located. It would have been a matter of a minute or two to drive there and take part in whatever scheme Danny James had cooked up. Helen frowned, her eyes fixed on a bright pink poster announcing a new bookstore opening up in Oakland. If only she could be more sure of Marita's innocence in this affair. She had a sudden thought that perhaps Donna Forsythe herself wasn't too sure either. Maybe that's what this was all about, rather than the protection of the Forsythe name.

"Hey, haven't we met before somewhere?" A warm breath tickled her ear. She whirled around to see Frieda behind her, all anger set aside for the moment.

"God, you scared me. How's it going over there?" Helen led Frieda to a booth, noticing that she was wearing Helen's favorite clothes — the red and gray silk tunic over black pants. She watched Frieda appreciatively, seeing how her lover's breasts strained against the fabric slightly as she reached behind her to drape her coat over the back of her seat. Frieda caught the look and smiled, as if knowing exactly what was going through Helen's mind.

Ellie, the new waitress, came to take their order. Helen leaned back in the booth and listened to Frieda talk about her show at the Women's Center. "It's been pretty busy," she was saying. "There's been a steady crowd since they opened the doors."

"No surprise to me," Helen said.

"All those eager students," Frieda went on with a sigh. "Makes me feel like a fossil, something in a museum. Asking me so many questions!"

"Don't laugh. All those young women — they give me nightmares." Helen felt a sudden twinge of remorse. "I don't know how I got so lucky."

Frieda smiled again. "Must have been the uniform. I never could resist a woman in a uniform."

As they waited for Ellie to bring them their lunch, Helen was strongly reminded of the first time she'd seen Frieda. It had been some kind of political demonstration — she couldn't remember for what —

65

and Frieda had been in the front of a noisy, confused crowd, shouting and chanting, her face alight with excitement. That was nearly ten years ago, Helen realized with a shock.

"What's the matter?" Frieda asked.

"I was just trying to remember what you were demonstrating for when we met the first time."

"Boycotting something or other, I think. I saw you right away. You were really cute."

"I wasn't feeling cute. All I could think of was how scared I was. All of you looked so brave and confident out there. I just kept hoping you wouldn't run right over me."

Frieda laughed. "Bet you wish you'd hauled me up into the paddy wagon with the rest! I knew it was love at first sight when you pushed me out of the way."

"Maybe you wish you hadn't invited me home that night."

"Well, it did raise a few eyebrows with my friends when they found out I was dating a cop," she said. "No regrets, though."

"How about a private eye?" Helen asked. "Is that any better than a cop in their opinion?"

Frieda looked down and started tapping her nails against her glass of water. "Better," she answered. "I think private eyes are seen as renegades, operating just this side of the law."

Helen kept herself from asking Frieda her own opinion, and fortunately Ellie chose that moment to set their plates in front of them. Helen looked at her salad with some trepidation. Whoever was in the kitchen today had piled it high with bean sprouts again. "Thanks," she said to Ellie with a bright smile. To Frieda, between clenched teeth, she muttered, "I hate these things."

"So, how's the case going?" Frieda asked abruptly.

"Fine. I have a lot of legwork to do." Helen wished fervently that Frieda hadn't asked, hadn't spoiled things. It was odd how any reference to her work made Helen defensive these days. Frieda was separate from it all, and Helen wanted to keep it that way. Whenever her lover asked her about the agency, it was as though a partition in her life was beginning to crack and chip, the dust settling in her eyes and lungs. Helen had always been good at dividing her life up into compartments. Into separate but equal areas. At least that was what she had always told herself. It was how she'd always lived. Sometimes, though, she envied Frieda's ability to live a single life, with everything all of a piece in her mind and her heart.

"Hey, wake up! You all right?"

"Sorry. I'm fine." Helen tackled the bean sprouts again with determination and tried to shut off her mind for a while.

Chapter 9

There was a message from Donna Forsythe on the answering machine when Helen arrived at her office. She was asking for news. "I'll be out tonight, but I'll try again in the morning," the recording told her.

Helen felt an inexplicable sense of relief at having missed her. She looked through her mail. Nothing much — a bill or two, a newspaper. The double murder at the bank had already fallen out of the papers — there was no mention of it to be found. Impatient to be doing something, Helen opened the file on the case and copied over her notes from the interview with Andre Spicer. Something big happening very soon, Danny James had said. She spread out all her notes on the table and her eyes fell on Marita's drawing of the timer. It was then that she got the idea. Deciding it was worth the risk of calling Marita at work, Helen dialed the number of Greater East Bay Bank.

"The alarm company?" Marita's surprise flowed over the line. "Just a second." Helen listened to Muzak for about a minute, then Marita was back. "The Dunham Alarm Company, on Post Street in San Francisco. The notice is posted right over the door —"

But Helen wasn't interested in that. "Thanks, Marita. See you tonight." If the timer was getting its regular servicing and cleaning the day of the break-in, she reasoned, maybe the service technician had noticed something. Anything.

The answer was prompt. "Dunham Alarm Company, Bill speaking."

"Service department, please . . . Hello, I'm a reporter with the *Berkeley Voice,*" she lied, pulling the name of a newspaper from her imagination and hoping the person on the other end didn't know any better. "We're doing a follow-up story on the murders at Greater East Bay Bank." She put on her bubbliest voice and was horrified, in spite of herself, at the ease with which she slipped into the role of a Southern belle.

The man on the other end hesitated. "Well, I don't know if I should —"

"Oh, it won't be talking about the alarms or anything," Helen said soothingly. "It's more a human interest kind of thing, you know, people's reactions to the violence around us, crime in our town, that sort of thing. I wanted to get a personal perspective from the people that were there right before it happened — customers, employees, service people."

"Hold on," the voice said, exasperated. Then she heard, shouted in the distance, "Hey, Larry! It's another newspaper calling!" There were assorted murmurings, then loud scratching noises.

"Hello? You wanted to talk to me?"

Helen went through her spiel again and found Larry only too glad to be in the limelight one more time. "Yeah, I was there that day. If you ask me it's one of them kids from the school that did it. Or gangs, maybe. What do they call 'em — Crips or something like that? You should see 'em wandering around all over the place looking like God knows what. Bunch of punks."

"And you were working on the alarm, Mr. —"

"Borden, Larry Borden. Yeah, that's right. Just the regular annual cleaning."

"What can you tell me about that day? Do you remember anything unusual happening while you were there?"

"No, not a damn thing. You coulda knocked me over with a feather when I saw it in the papers the next day."

Helen's heart sank as she let him rant on about kids today and the difficulties of his job until something he said caught her attention. "Could you repeat that, Mr. Borden?"

"I said, maybe if the cops figure out who killed this guy they could find my tools for me, too."

She froze. "Your tools are missing?"

"Well, not exactly. See, I was working on that

timer there at the bank? And I got the clock all taken apart and cleaned up, then I turned around to find my screwdriver gone. It's this special one, a real little Phillips, and nothing else I have will fit their clock. That whole building is falling apart right now, everything's so old they don't make parts —"

"But the screwdriver. It's gone?"

"I'm trying to tell you. It was really weird. I had to use it to get the face off the clock, and then I turned around and it was gone. Damndest thing you ever saw. I looked all over for it, but it was just plain gone. So I went back out to the truck to see if I could find something else. Like I said, it's the only one I had. When I didn't find another one, I went back inside, thinking maybe someone there at the bank had a tool kit or something. So what do you think happened?"

"I have no idea."

"There it was, right where I left it! Right there on top of my box. Now, how do you explain that one?"

"I don't suppose you noticed anyone hanging around the vault when you got back?"

"Are you kidding? Those gals are all over the place all the time. They weren't paying any attention to me."

"Mr. Borden, did you tell this to the police?"

"No way! All I need is for them to go off and talk to my boss about it. I get enough hassles from him. He's always on my ass about being careless, but if he could see what all I have to put up with in these places —"

Helen cut his complaints short. "Thank you very much, Mr. Borden. You've been very helpful."

71

"Hey, no problem. When do you think I'll see my name in the paper? What paper was it, anyway?"

"Oh, soon, very soon. Goodbye, Mr. Borden. And thanks again." She hung up, thinking hard, as he was asking her name. It would only have taken a second or two to adjust the face of the clock and Larry Borden sounded more worried about his boss discovering his carelessness than about who was messing around with the alarm.

She suddenly felt great impatience to go to the bank herself. Helen got up and prepared to lock up the office. She could stop by the house and feed Boobella before the Chamber of Commerce party, then go and just look at the area around the bank before going in. When she got home, she saw a note from Frieda slipped inside the front door: "Went out for supper with some people from the university. I'll stop by later. Love, Frieda." So that was that. Helen took the note inside with her to the kitchen and placed it in a drawer where she kept everything Frieda had ever written to her. Frieda herself didn't know of the existence of the drawer.

After Boobella's accusations of malicious starvation had been assuaged, Helen went to her bedroom and searched her closet. Presumably a Chamber of Commerce gathering would be a rather conservative affair. She ought to change her pants and get into something more appropriate. At least she'd kept her good pin-stripe suit. It had been tailored for her, and the dark blue would certainly not be too showy. A memory of Donna Forsythe's immaculate gray sailed before her eyes as she made one final check in the mirror. "What do you think?" she asked Boobella, who watched her solemnly.

A few minutes later she turned onto College Avenue, glad that she'd gotten an early start. The traffic near the bank was quite busy as she drove around looking for a place to park. Rush hour was just beginning, and the sun was on its way down behind the hills. Helen finally nudged her car into a space two blocks down from College Avenue.

As she got out of the car, pulling her coat more closely about her, she felt a wave of nostalgia. This was the Berkeley she'd fallen in love with when she'd first left Mississippi all those years ago. It was difficult to explain, even to Aunt Josephine, who'd always preferred living in San Francisco. "Why go all the way out there?" she'd ask from the cozy security of her apartment in the Marina district, near Golden Gate. "It's not safe, with all that wild stuff happening at the campus. You better stay here with me." But Helen had refused. The sudden change from the languorous, humid air of Mississippi to the cool wind and the morning fog had seemed intoxicating to Helen. She could recall her own student days with great fondness on a night like this. The people passing her on the sidewalks, scurrying to get home, were a grab-bag of types — students worried about final exams, older people who still looked like students, a handful of leftovers from Haight-Ashbury who'd drifted east across the bay. Not too many tourists this time of year since football season was over. The street had a feel of life and activity, and Helen was grateful she could still absorb it. In this jaunty mood she crossed College and approached the bank.

It was a charming building, set back from the street with a flagstone walkway leading up to the front doors through flower beds that were now bare. The yellow exterior looked mellowed rather than garish, as though weathered with time and the seasons. The windows were shielded by shutters instead of blinds, and the roof was shingled. It looked more like someone's large old home than a financial institution.

Walking closer, Helen wondered how visible it would be in the kind of thick fog they'd been having lately. Since the murder took place between midnight and one in the morning, the building would very likely have been completely shrouded at that time. It was far enough from the residential area where she'd parked for any noises to go unheard. Even if they had been heard, Helen had lived in Berkeley long enough to know that odd noises were a part of life there, and most people schooled themselves not to pay too much attention to them. Moreover, the shops on either side of the bank — a bookstore and a dry cleaners — would have been deserted long before anything happened.

Helen went around to the back of the bank, where a tiny parking lot was tucked away. It was completely filled. Through the back door of the building she could see a huge Christmas tree, placed squarely in front of the door, blocking her view of anything inside the lobby. Stepping back, she looked up to the second story. One window, high up on the wall, perhaps opening into a bathroom or storeroom, was fastened shut against the cold. The rest of the wall was a sheer drop to the ground.

On the other side of the lot, some kind of construction work was going on. Helen couldn't make out what was going up there. Then she saw the large sign posted in front of the site. It proclaimed that this would be a new parking building for the city, due to be completed in July of the following year. She walked around the perimeter, stepping cautiously in the growing darkness. Past the construction site there were several clumps of trees, and beyond them she could see more houses.

She was just wondering if anyone in the houses could have seen anything when she heard a raspy whisper behind her.

"Are you washed in the blood of the lamb, lady?"

Her heart stopped and she whipped around. "What — what did you say?"

"I ast you if you was washed in the blood of the lamb." He was very dirty and very old. His greasy white hair stuck out from under a moth-eaten brown ski cap. The rest of his body was swathed in several layers of filthy garments, the outer layer consisting of a padded Oriental jacket and torn corduroy trousers with ragged hems. Oddly enough, his feet bore new shoes, probably a recent acquisition. They fit badly, causing him to shuffle, crablike.

Regaining her breath, Helen answered, "I doubt it, but you never know."

He shook his greasy head, muttering to himself. "I thought you must be one of 'em. I guess not."

"One of what?"

"It don't matter none, lady. My mistake. They'll come back one of these days, maybe." With a courtly bow, he turned away and went back toward the street. His backpack, stuffed to the bursting point, bobbed up and down as he slid along. Now and then the canvas flap on the pack flapped open to give passersby a glimpse of the wadded worldly goods it contained.

Helen stood there watching him until she felt the cold seeping into her coat. Time to go in, anyway, she thought. Hoping no one had seen her poking around she followed the old man's path to the street and headed for the front door of the bank.

Chapter 10

The front door was open. Helen walked into a confusing scene. People were arranged around the tree as if around a centerpiece, talking in groups. Some were hanging ornaments, but most were eating and drinking and pretending not to look in the direction of the vault. Helen could see it from where she stood, its polished metal gleaming dully in the soft light. The stainless steel door had been locked up for the night, and the large combination dial was visible just to the right of the spoked wheel in the center.

"Helen," she heard. It was Marita, standing next to the tree and holding a silver garland. Two other women stood in tableau with her, each holding decorations. Helen approached them, careful not to tread on the boxes splayed on the floor.

Marita said hello with an anxious smile. Helen noticed a great change in her attire today. She was wearing a simple skirt and blouse, and small stud earrings sparkled out from the black hair. The change also included her manner. She was much more ill-at-ease here than she'd been last night. The other two women were studying her quite frankly. The older of the two was puffing on a cigarette and staring through thick glasses at a styrofoam angel that dangled precariously on a high branch of the tree. Evelyn Mayes, Helen thought, and the other girl might be Mattie Wilson. Mattie was wearing an ill-fitting short dress of orange, which was the worst color she could have chosen. Her sullen expression clashed sharply with the occasion.

Introductions proved Helen's guesses correct. "Helen is an old friend of mine," Marita was saying. Helen merely smiled and watched the others. "I've always received notices about these gatherings in the mail at my office, of course, but I've never attended one before."

"Where's that? Your office, I mean," Evelyn asked without glancing down.

"Over on Shattuck Avenue, near the campus."

"Welcome to Santa's workshop," Mattie said in a voice that matched her expression. "I'd advise you to get a drink. You'll need it before the evening's over."

"Actually, I could use one," Helen said evenly, her

smile never breaking. Marita guided her through the crowd to a buffet table, where they both helped themselves. Marita babbled a bit, loudly and nervously, waiting for a couple of middle-aged men in suits to move out of earshot.

"You're not going to tell them you're a detective, are you?"

"It's better for now," Helen answered, consciously putting reassurance in her voice. "Tonight I'd just like to watch things a bit."

As they talked Helen let her eyes travel over the room until they rested on the vault door, visible from any part of the room. It was in the far right corner at the rear of the building, discreetly tucked away behind the paneled half-door all banks had to separate the tellers' line, narrow as a ship's galley, from the rest of the lobby. She saw what must be Marita's desk next to the wall in front of the vault, as Manny's notes had described. The vault itself was smaller and less imposing than she'd imagined. It looked more like a large walk-in closet with an oddly elaborate door.

"There's Lucille," Marita was saying, and Helen turned her gaze in the direction indicated. A middle-aged woman with graying blonde hair in a tight permanent wave was holding a small plate of untouched food and watching a group of people throwing tinsel at the tree with more hilarity than accuracy. Helen guessed that she was having a hard time restraining herself from picking the stray silver threads from the carpet before they became embedded there. Her white polyester sweater hung loosely on her as though she'd recently lost weight.

"Hey, Janet!" They heard Evelyn call a greeting to another young woman who joined Mattie at the tree. "Is Dave coming?"

A slight wince flickered over Janet Strosser's carefully made-up face, and her long, blood-red fingernails froze for a moment over the gold star she was holding. "He may show up. He said he had appointments this afternoon." A forced smile played over her lips that had too much lipstick smeared on. Carrying plates, Helen and Marita slowly made their way back to the tree to join the others.

"Oh, God, get a load of this," Mattie groaned, twisting her mouth in disgust. She pushed her lank brown hair out of her eyes with pudgy fingers and then gestured to the front of the building. An extremely pretty blonde girl, wearing a tight black miniskirt and a low-cut red silk blouse, was laughing and smiling near the front door for the benefit of a handful of very interested men. They were, against her giggling protests, pretending to hang various ornaments on her clothing and drape her with tinsel and garlands. She teetered on red spiked heels as they spun her this way and that.

Evelyn just smiled and shook her head and continued her search for more angels. Janet was too absorbed in untangling ornament hooks to notice. Mattie, however, stared with loathing. "Must be Lorie Harris," Helen said in a soft voice, and Marita nodded.

The scene was interrupted by the entrance of a tall, thin man whose head was covered by a luxuriant growth of white hair. He wore a khaki parka, which was greatly at odds with his well-cut gray suit. His attache case overflowed with files and papers.

"That's the auditor, Ed Grant," Marita told Helen. They watched him edge past Lorie and her entourage, uncertainly setting his briefcase against the wall. Ed looked around a moment, lost, then advanced toward a balding pink-faced man who was noisily greeting some newcomers with great joviality.

"And that's the manager, Mr. Neely."

"Ed! Didn't think you were gonna make it!" Jerry Neely slapped the white-haired man on the back with his free hand. The other hand balanced a plastic cup full of punch, sloshing around and spilling onto the carpet.

"Well, Jerry, I did want to make sure these files got back here tonight."

"Come on, take off that coat and get something to drink. Goddamn, man, you look like you're dressed for a duck hunt," Mr. Neely boomed. Reluctantly, Ed unzipped the parka and laid it over a nearby chair, accepting the glass of eggnog forced on him.

"I really can't stay, Jerry." He took a sip of the eggnog and tried to disguise his distaste. "Gladys is expecting me home."

"Nonsense! We gotta loosen you up a little, that's all that's the matter with you!" Jerry kept patting him on the back and trying to guide him over to the table. "Now, you gotta try this fruitcake —" He reached over and groped for a plate, brushing against Ed as he did so. "It's just about the best —"

"Jerry, be careful! Oh for Christ's sake!" Ed suddenly yelped as Mr. Neely's eager hands bumped against the glass of eggnog, and the creamy yellow liquid dribbled down the gray suit.

Jerry was all fumbles and apologies as he lurched

around looking for napkins. "Sorry, Ed. Just got clumsy for a minute. Here, lemme —"

"No, no!" Ed flung off Jerry's assistance. "You'll just rub it in."

"Well, maybe we could use a little water."

"That will just set the stain, Jerry. Never mind. It'll have to go to the cleaners now," Ed informed him peevishly.

Helen thought of the office parties she had attended in the past with the other men and women working in homicide. This was by comparison a very sedate crowd. Was it the daily dealing in life-and-death situations that made her old buddies on the police force more uninhibited, more prepared to get smashed and behave like fools? Undoubtedly there was just as much tension here among the employees. Perhaps the knowledge that any day she and her friends could have been blown to bits out on the streets made the difference in the gatherings she could recall.

"Barrel of laughs, isn't he?" Marita asked, referring to Ed Grant with a nod. "Believe me, he acts the same about the audit as he does about his clothes."

"What the hell is he doing here, anyway?" Mattie growled. She had made a trip to the refreshment table and Helen watched her pop cookies and bits of cake into her mouth in quick succession, holding the plate close to her chin.

"Maybe Mr. Neely thought we'd get a good audit this year if we invited him to our party," Marita answered.

"You think so?" Evelyn asked, giving up on the decorations and pulling a cigarette out of her purse,

82

which lay open on the floor. "I think maybe Mr. Neely just feels sorry for him. You know, with that wife of his. Have you ever seen her?"

"Once," Marita said after she finished her drink. "She was able to stand up on her own that time. I hear she got really bombed at the company picnic last summer, dancing around and trying to flirt with every man in sight. It's really disgusting."

"Well," Mattie sighed, putting her empty plate down with regret, "if I had to wake up next to old fart-face every morning I'd probably start drinking, too."

At that moment Jerry Neely called out for everyone's attention, announcing that he was about to turn off the lights so they could see the tree in all its glory. The crowd by the refreshment tables stood still in vague expectation during one last search for extension cords and light bulbs. Finally all was ready.

"Okay, here goes!" For the period of about a minute, the room was plunged into complete darkness. After the light and the noise of the crowd Helen felt disoriented. Then the colored lights of the tree began to twinkle red, then green, then blue, and an intake of breath, suitably awed, sounded throughout the room. The tree winked and glowed in true Christmas fashion, while the rest of the room reflected its soft light.

After a few moments of admiration, Jerry threw the switch again, and everyone blinked and looked foolish and said how beautiful it was. No one was ready to go just yet. The food and drink were still drawing a crowd. Helen excused herself from Marita and began to wander. No one paid too much attention to her, partly because she kept in motion, never stopping long enough to get involved in conversation.

She wandered with a purpose, however. Her mind was still on Lorie, standing in the midst of her admirers. She'd seen the girl before. In fact, Helen had seen her earlier that day, hours ago, in Andre Spicer's apartment. At that time, she'd been looking out from a web of black lace, in one of Danny James' pictures.

Chapter 11

Helen went back to the refreshment table for another drink. As she waited her turn at the punch bowl, she saw Lucille Ogden, the operations officer, standing in the dimly lit foyer by the back door. She picked absently at the fruitcake on her paper plate, staring down at the floor. Helen refilled her cup and went quietly into the foyer.

Lucille barely noticed her presence. "The tree certainly looks beautiful," Helen started. "It's awfully tall, though. You must have had a hard time getting it in here."

But Lucille didn't respond. She just kept staring at the carpet. Helen followed her gaze and saw an oddly shaped stain next to the operations officer's flat-heeled shoes. The woman murmured something, too low for Helen to hear.

"What was that?" Helen leaned in a little closer.

"This was where it happened," Lucille answered. Where poor Bob — where they found him. They said his eyes were open." Her thin, tightly drawn lips trembled. Helen was afraid she'd break down completely. Glancing around quickly she spotted a couple of cushioned chairs next to an imposing mahogany desk.

"Here, let's sit down over here. I'll get you another drink, all right?" Helen hurried back to the table and noticed that Marita was watching her, but she didn't want to talk. She sped back to Lucille with a cup of wine punch. The other woman sipped, holding the cup with a shaky hand.

"Better now?" Helen asked.

"Yes, thanks," and she managed a smile, then looked away quickly. "It just seemed so awful for a moment — all of us having a good time, and Bob barely cold. I called his wife yesterday. She's in a terrible state." Her voice was growing stronger. A couple of other people nearby overheard a1d looked around curiously. Lucille went on, "I wish they'd replace that carpet. I just can't stand walking in every morning, looking at it."

"Maybe you could make a special request," Helen suggested.

"Oh, it's probably not necessary. This place is falling apart, actually. We're due for a remodeling next year." Lucille sipped again and seemed calmer.

The onlookers went away once they realized that nothing much was going to happen, but Helen noticed Jerry strolling in their direction with a concerned expression. He had heard Lucille's last comment.

"I'd sure like to see some touchtone phones and electric typewriters," he drawled cheerily. He reached to the desk behind and tapped on the ancient Olivetti resting on the scarred surface. "Can you believe they still expect us to use these things?"

Helen examined her surroundings more closely. Up to that point she'd been observing the people. Now, following the gaze of her companions, she was forced to agree with their complaints. The old furniture and floral carpets looked quaint when seen in the glow of Christmas lights, but they were clearly wearing thin, eroding and fading under the harsh fluorescent lights. The table that held the refreshments was a good one, she noted, as was the desk in the corner, but they too had suffered from too many years of industrial cleanings. It would all fit with what Marita had told her about the dilapidated state of the vault's time mechanism — another point acting in the killer's favor.

Lucille's sniffles interrupted her musing, and Helen tactfully left her in the kindly, albeit clumsy, hands of Mr. Neely. Lucille Ogden, Helen thought, was the only person here who seemed genuinely disturbed by the incident. There might be more here than met the eye. Helen decided to check up on Lucille later.

Right now the other employees of the bank were huddled around the Christmas tree, whispering and glancing in Lucille's direction. Helen walked up to them and stood next to Marita.

Evelyn was poking around under the tree. "Where the hell did my cigarettes go? Oh, there's my purse," and she emerged triumphantly clutching the cellophane package. "Poor thing," she clucked, looking over at Lucille and Jerry. "This whole thing has hit her really hard."

"Well, I don't know why we don't just come out in the open and talk about it," Janet exclaimed, folding her arms tightly across her chest and drumming her long nails on her arms. "Why else do you think all these fine upstanding citizens came here tonight? For stale cookies and spiked punch?"

"Janet's right," Mattie agreed. She had another plateful of cake and still ate as though she were starved. "It's just like drivers slowing down on the freeway to get a closer look at an accident. I know," she said, suddenly brightening. "We could open up the vault and give everyone a guided tour. We could even charge admission, raise some money."

"Should we use tape recorders or have guides, Mattie?" Marita asked, laughing.

"Why, of course, Lorie should be our designated guide," Janet said, a malicious smile settling on her cracked lips. "She's our star attraction, after all."

Helen saw Mattie's face darken, and Janet stepped back from what she had started. Marita and Evelyn turned away in irritation. Their expressions told Helen that Janet was only stirring the pot. This was some kind of long-standing feud.

Lorie had heard her name, and she turned around from her suitors to see Mattie glowering at her. She stalked over to the tree unsteadily. Helen could tell she'd probably had more than enough punch for one evening.

"What are you guys talking about?"

"Oh, nothing," Janet sang out. "Mattie's just kind of upset to see you having such a good time when we should all be in mourning."

"What's that supposed to mean?" Lorie asked. She looked contemptuously at Mattie.

"Come on, now." Evelyn tried to intervene, but Lorie wasn't ready to stop. She saw Mattie's red face and angry eyes.

"There she goes again, folks, trying so hard to be a good influence," Lorie sighed, moving closer to Mattie. "Has to try to piss me off because she's jealous."

"Jealous?" Mattie spat out, dropping her plate on the floor. "Of you? That's just the sort of stupid thing you would say. I wouldn't push it if I were you. Not with everything that's been going on lately."

Lorie closed her eyes and leaned against a chair in mock weariness. "Will someone kindly take this girl home to mother?" she asked.

But Mattie ignored the words. She leaned over and spoke right in Lorie's face. "Why don't you just shut up? Shut your big fat stupid mouth!"

"I suppose you're going to make me?"

Mattie suddenly got a huge smile on her face. She leered grotesquely at the other woman. "Maybe it'll make you shut up if I tell everyone here what you used to do on the weekends. Up until last Thursday, that is. How about that, Lorie? How would you like these people to know that?"

Mattie got more of a reaction than she'd bargained for. Lorie's face went white and she held the back of the chair tightly. Mattie unconsciously backed away, scared now, her mouth falling open.

"You shut that fat mouth, you stupid hog," Lorie said in a steely, quiet voice. Jerry had by now left Lucille by the desk and was looking around in a state of helplessness at the tense group. He glanced back at Lucille, beseeching her to do something about all this. Her help wasn't necessary, however, for Mattie turned away, her face red and bloated, and left the tree. They all watched her grab a coat from the pile on the counter and wait by the front door for the new security guard to let her out.

"Nice going, Janet," Evelyn sighed, lighting a cigarette. She stubbed out her last one in a sand-filled ashtray, pushing it in deep with yellow-stained fingers. "You just had to do it one more time, didn't you?"

"That was disgusting," Marita muttered, with a glance at Helen to see what she thought of it all.

"Who, me, coach?" Janet looked around with wide innocent eyes and wandered off, satisfied.

"Hell, we're all about ready to snap these days," Evelyn said, exhaling a stream of blue smoke. "I just wish they'd get this damn thing over with and arrest somebody. Hey, where's my lighter?"

"Janet's right about one thing, though," Marita said, moving away from the tree. Helen followed her until they were out of hearing range of the others. "I think we need to quit pretending nothing happened, at least among ourselves," she continued.

"Excuse me a minute, Marita," Helen said. She saw that Lorie was back at the punch bowl, alone this time, and Helen wanted a chance to talk to her.

Lorie looked up at Helen with bleary eyes. The near-brawl under the tree had drained her, somehow. She propped herself up with one hand and emptied the glass with one gulp, then shook the hair from her eyes. "May I help you?" she asked Helen sarcastically.

"You know, I think I've seen you before," Helen said.

"I don't think so," Lorie answered. She looked Helen over with a scowl.

"Oh yes, I have."

"Where?"

"In some photographs."

All the anger disappeared from Lorie's face. Now she was just afraid. "I don't know what you're talking about," she said, stumbling a little on her high heels.

"I think you do," Helen responded.

"What do you want?" Lorie whispered through stiff lips.

"I just want to talk to you about it." Helen reached into her shoulder bag and found her card case. "This is my card, Lorie. Please use it and give me a call tomorrow."

"Are you going to talk to Marita, too?"

Helen managed to control her surprise as she answered vaguely, "I'll be talking to a lot of people in the next few days. I hope you're one of them." She offered the card again.

Lorie finally took it and turned it over in her hands. "You're crazy. I have nothing to say to you." She ripped the card in half and threw it to the floor.

"Sleep on it. Maybe you'll feel differently tomorrow." Helen turned and walked away, unwilling to see or hear any more. Marita found her as she was looking for her coat.

"Are you going already?"

"There's really nothing else I can do tonight, Marita. I'll call you soon." The guard opened the door for her, and Helen went out quickly, taking deep lungfuls of cold air as she headed for her car. As she walked, she heard something. Moaning? Crying? No, it was more cadenced than that. Singing, she decided. Someone was singing out there in the dark and the fog. And it was a song she remembered, from her childhood.

"Are you washed in the blood of the lamb?"

Chapter 12

No, she wasn't mistaken. It really was someone singing in a wavering voice: *"Are your garments spotless, are they white as snow, are you washed in the blood of the lamb?"*

Something in the voice reminded her of the old man she'd seen earlier, the one who'd startled her in the parking lot. It was pitch dark and foggy. As she slowly made her way around the building, she wished she'd brought a flashlight with her. Her foot stubbed up against something that rattled slightly as she neared the construction site next to the parking area.

It was a row of planks used to shore up some loose earth. Helen leaned over this makeshift bulwark and cautiously groped around the edges of the wood. Someone had dug a sort of hollow in the dirt at one end, using the planks as a support. As she reached out she heard a scuffling noise.

"I ain't done nothin', lady! Don't hurt me! I was just goin' —" He was scooping up a blanket or covering, his hands scraping the clay dirt. His eyes veered wildly away from meeting hers in the filtered light from the street lamps. "I wan't stayin' here, honest."

"Hey, hey, calm down. It's okay. Remember me? I was here a little earlier." She climbed carefully over the planks, crouching down low. As her eyes grew accustomed to the darkness, she saw that he'd set up a sort of nest here. His few belongings were carefully arranged at his side — a plastic bag containing bread and a jelly jar; a dilapidated King James Bible, missing its spine; an enameled mug holding a bent and tarnished spoon. The hideaway was close and fusty, in spite of its being exposed to the elements on all sides. It was a scent she suspected the old man carried with him wherever he went. She'd smelled worse.

"I'm sorry I disturbed you. Was that you singing just now?" He still looked terrified, but Helen could tell he might be thawing to her, perhaps because she had chosen to kneel down beside him rather than talk down to him from beyond the planks. "I'm Helen. What's your name?"

"Ben," he mumbled.

"Do you sleep out here often, Ben? Looks like it can be pretty cozy here, out of the wind."

He nodded. " 'Ceptin' sometimes when it rains. I don't ast for nothin' though. The Lord will provide."

"That's what the Lord said, all right. I guess he provided you with this place, didn't he?"

"You're no police, I can tell that," he burst out. He began to snicker softly. "When you was out there before —" He pointed to the parking lot. "I wasn't sure, but I knowed you musta come for the blood of the lamb."

Helen, steeling herself to breathe the acrid atmosphere Ben lived in, moved a little closer. "Ben, do you remember a night a while ago when someone else was out here? Two people, maybe, that went inside this building and then only one came out?"

"You mean in there with them usurers?" He stuck out a bony finger and gestured to the back door. His long fingernails crooked out in accusation. "You know what the Lord said about their kind? Said they was all damned to hellfire! Put not your faith in what wasteth away but into everlasting life! Jesus our savior cast out the moneychangers from the temple. It was a sign of the end, all that blood. He sent his angel of death in there, lady."

He leaned closer to her and she forced herself to stay still, not to flinch and back off from the sour smell of unwashed hair and fetid, heavy breath. "They too shall be judged and found wanting when the Lord separates the sheep from the goats. Already the winnowing fan is out and he will use it. The first shall be last and the last shall be first."

He staggered up and stretched his hands out, over the embankment, into the fog. "Come Lord Jesus!"

Helen sighed. She was tired and this was getting nowhere. She was just wondering if she should leave him some money when he said, "Don't matter how much them cops keep runnin' around, lookin' for what went in there that night. It weren't no man. It was God's own angel of death!"

"The angel of death hit the security guard over the head?" Nod. "Did you see the angel, Ben?" Another nod.

Helen shifted so that she was sitting more comfortably upon the cold earth. "What did the angel look like?"

"He walked in a cloud of glory and then was taken up, lady," he whispered in reverent awe. "Police can't catch no angel of death, you know. Not unless God wants him caught." He abruptly started to cackle, wheezing with a gleeful expression on his grimy face, and slapped his knee at the thought. "Them cops goin' here and goin' there like they was after some mere mortal. Pretty crazy, ain't it?"

"Was it a man or a woman?"

"There ain't no man nor woman in heaven. We're all one, shining, glorious being there."

"That's nice, Ben," she said, but he ignored her and went on with his vision.

"The angel walked by here in a cloud of glory, and this became holy ground."

"The angel walked by you? Did you see its face?"

"He carried gifts of the holy spirit in his arms, wrapped up in a bundle." He showed her, putting his arms out in a circle in front of him. "Then I was slain in the spirit and knew no more."

"Gifts," Helen repeated. The killer carried something out with him, something wrapped up. "What happened to the gifts, Ben?" Maybe it was money, or some kind of valuable item that had been stored in the vault.

But Ben suddenly became suspicious. "I don't know, lady," he answered sullenly. "I told you, I don't remember nothin' else." He began to pack up his belongings, cramming them into an already overstuffed backpack.

"But did you see the gifts, Ben?" She scrambled after him, anxious not to lose him. "Ben?"

He turned and stood, a small black hunched figure, dark in the milky fog. He spoke to her sternly. "Do not look upon the face of Jehovah, or ye shall die! I couldn't look up, no one can look at the face of Yahweh. I hid over there and waited." He pointed behind her to the hideaway. "Then I seen the light and knowed what it meant."

"What, Ben? What did it mean?"

"It meant that I was on holy ground! Yessir, a sign from the Lord's own angel that I was now one of the elect, for only I have seen him here!"

Ben had walked back to the hideaway as he spoke, and Helen could see the rabid gleam in his eyes. "Did the police talk to you, Ben? Did they come here and ask you about any of this?" She could just see Lieutenant Haskell trying to be patient with someone like Ben.

He cackled again. "Sure, lady, they ast me things. But the Lord works in mysterious ways, and I ain't gonna tell on him. Not now that I'm one of the chosen."

"I doubt very much if the Lord had anything to do with what happened in there that night, Ben," Helen said, casting her thoughts about for a way to keep him talking. "Maybe," she ventured, "maybe I'm one of the elect, too, Ben. After all, the Lord could have led me here to his holy ground. And to you." Thank God Manny can't see me here, Helen thought. It would be all over the station by tomorrow.

Ben muttered. He was still uncertain. "Well, I don't know yet. You might just be another of them infidels. I can't tell if you been washed in the blood." He started to walk away, shaking his head, ignoring Helen's attempts to stumble after him in the dark. He knew his way, unlike Helen, and she soon lost him in the fog.

Helen followed slowly, looking back at the building, trying to visualize what Ben must have seen. The bank was dark now. The party must have broken up soon after she'd gone. Helen walked across the parking lot. He'd seen someone going down the steps at the back door of the bank, carrying something. She still wasn't too sure if Ben had witnessed the killing of the guard, but the old man had definitely seen the killer come back out of the bank. She stood now on the small porch at the back door. What would the killer have seen, standing here? Well, first, the construction site, looming up a few yards away. It was an excellent place to dispose of evidence, since it was likely that anything concealed there would be buried under several tons of concrete soon enough. She went back to the spot where she'd first seen Ben and skirted the edge of the parking lot that joined the street. There were some piles of bricks, planks in stacks according to size, large sacks, a dumpster — too easy. Besides, the police would have checked it already.

Passing headlights in the distant street caught her

eye and made her realize the lateness of the hour. She would come back some other time, perhaps very early in the morning, when there was better light. The thought of Frieda possibly waiting up for her made her hurry to her car.

She wasn't disappointed. The day's events, although not really physically demanding, had drained Helen of all energy. She was more exhausted today than she had been in months. She found Frieda asleep in bed, her long dark hair a tangled knot on the pillow, her face hidden. Helen moved softly so as to not wake her. As Helen got under the sheets, Frieda stirred, turned, reached out to her unconsciously. Her head sought and then nestled on Helen's breast and she sighed. As she stroked Frieda's smooth back Helen had a sudden image of Ben huddled out somewhere in the cold wet streets of Berkeley. She hoped he had returned to the hideaway by now. Holding Frieda tighter, Helen drifted into an uneasy sleep.

Chapter 13

Helen was awakened the next morning by Frieda. The bed shook as Frieda sat down on it awkwardly. She was balancing two cups of coffee and the morning paper. Helen struggled to wake up, forcing her heavy eyelids open. The coffee smelled good.

"What time is it?" Helen asked, yawning. She saw now that Frieda was already wearing her leather jacket and wool scarf. "Where are you going?"

"I have to meet Dianne at the gallery in the city today," Frieda answered as she handed Helen a cup. "I'll probably be gone all day."

"Oh." Helen drank gratefully. "Thanks. It's good coffee." Something was wrong. Frieda sat tensely, her arms held close to her sides and her legs stuck straight out on the bed. Helen knew it was better to go ahead and get it over with. "Are you going to tell me what's bugging you?" she asked.

"You don't even remember, do you?"

"Remember what?"

"Where you were going to spend a few minutes yesterday."

Shit, Helen thought, closing her eyes and leaning back on the pillows. The exhibit. Absorbed with the Danny James murder, Helen had completely forgotten about it. "Oh, Frieda, I'm so sorry. I meant to go —"

But Frieda had already moved off the bed. She said over her shoulder, "We'll talk about it tonight. See you later," and she was gone. The front door was closed a moment later carefully and quietly, but it might as well have been slammed. Helen didn't even think of going out to talk to her, to try to stop her. It was so obviously futile.

Instead, she relaxed under the covers and thought about Frieda. Helen knew that in many important ways, she was different from Frieda. Frieda was always sensitive to the feelings of others, always aware of what was going on around her. Helen, on the other hand, tended to focus on one thing or one person and let her mind become occupied, excluding all other distractions. That was what had happened yesterday. Helen silently raged at herself for a few moments. This exhibit had been very important to Frieda, and she, Helen, should have made more of an effort to be there. But the case was important, too. Helen had been floundering for six months in that

101

expensive office on Shattuck Avenue, watching Aunt Josephine's money slowly trickle away. She couldn't afford to blow this one.

Helen was glad to interrupt her train of unhappy thoughts by answering the telephone. Its loud ringing by her ear jolted her fully awake. She was glad when the voice of her ex-partner greeted her.

"Rise and shine," Manny sang out. He was a morning person, too, Helen remembered with disgust.

"What the hell do you want?"

"Is that gratitude? I risk getting my ass chopped off just to get you some information. I swear, hell hath no fury like an ungrateful child."

"You're mixing Shakespeare and Congreve."

"Huh?"

"Never mind. What have you got?"

"Well, it looks like our friend Danny boy is going to be a blind alley for us poor slobs in narcotics. Too small of a potato. Still, I did find out something that might interest you."

"Go on."

"Get this — he used to work for Greater East Bay Bank. About ten years ago, in the very same department with two of the names on the list I gave you. Lucille Ogden and Jerry Neely."

"You're not serious. What the hell did he do there?"

"He worked in their main Oakland office, in the wire transfer department. He would have been in his late twenties, then. He must have known both those people, Helen."

"Wait a minute, wait a minute. How on earth did

a bank hire him, with a record like his? Surely they check these things out."

"No, his rap sheet starts right after this. He was only with the bank for six months. His prints were on file with the feds for the bank employment, but he was working for a temporary agency at the time. Greater East Bay Bank took him on to do some filing when they were short-handed."

"Well, why didn't Lucille or Jerry say anything about it when they just happened to find his corpse in their vault? Seems like an obvious kind of thing to blurt out."

"I don't know. You can't really hold them to remembering something that happened for a month or two ten years ago."

"No, I guess not. It doesn't mean they've forgotten, though. Manny, I owe you another one. Thanks."

"Hold on! One other thing." She heard him shuffling papers and muttering curses in Spanish. Then, "Okay, here it is. They finally let me see the inventory of the vault contents. They found something missing."

"What?"

"You won't believe this, either. A whopping two hundred bucks. In twenties."

"You're right. I don't believe it."

"It's a fact. There was eighty thousand in twenties sealed up in a bag to be shipped out to the federal reserve in San Francisco that Friday. As soon as the agents from the FBI got in there after the discovery of the bodies, the manager, Neely, ran in to take a look at the bag. It had been cut open and the two hundred taken out. And that's all, folks."

Helen was silent for a moment as she absorbed this information. "Well, it doesn't make much sense yet, Manny. Thanks anyway, though."

"All right, get some more beauty sleep. You'd better be looking good for the funeral. You're going to be there, aren't you?"

"Whose funeral?"

"For Danny boy! Hopkins Memorial, here in Berkeley. Apparently his folks came out from Fresno."

"What time is the funeral?"

"Twelve-thirty. Get your best duds on."

"Manny, for a male of the species, you're not too bad."

Manny laughed. "And we all know what you think of men. See you around, Watson."

In a mood of excitement, Helen drove to the office about an hour later. Donna Forsythe was waiting for her in the hall outside the office door. "I was just about to leave you a note," she said, following her inside. "I've been wanting to talk to you. Is Marita all right?"

Helen had felt an inexplicable sense of impatience upon seeing Donna, but it went away when she saw the woman's stricken face. She was pale, and there were dark circles under her eyes. "Yes, she's fine," Helen answered.

Donna sat down heavily in the same chair she'd chosen before. "I haven't heard from her since the day before yesterday. What have you found out?"

"Enough to believe that drugs had little to do with this murder." Helen told her client about Danny

104

James' hints of a major event in his career of crime associated with the bank, leaving out any mention of the photographs of Lorie she'd seen.

"So Marita's private life won't be examined too closely?"

"I can't stop the homicide unit from doing its job, Ms. Forsythe, but I'd say you appear to be safe for the time being."

"Don't sit there and judge me," she snapped, turning a bright red. "I'm not paying you to do that."

"No one's making judgments here," Helen answered in a quiet voice. "I'm merely passing along information I thought you wanted."

Donna watched Helen for a moment and apparently decided that Helen didn't mean to be sarcastic. She asked, "And what about Marita's brother? Does he know anything about what happened?"

"Hard to say. Part of me is inclined to believe he's lying about something, but I don't know what. If the police are centering the investigation on the Oakland drug traffic, then they're likely to keep close tabs on Andre because of his record."

"Which means close tabs on Marita." Donna frowned. "If there were just some way to avoid that. Isn't there anyone you could talk to?"

Helen shook her head. "Who? The dealers? They'd just as soon kill me as look at me, especially since I was one of the enemy."

Suddenly Donna rose from her chair and began pacing the room. "Not if you had money. Not if you paid them enough."

"What are you talking about?"

"How much would these dealers want in cash before they'd talk to you about Danny James?"

Helen stared. "You don't have any idea what you're talking about. These people would have absolutely no trouble blowing your brains out on the least provocation. I won't let you even think about this. It's insane."

But Donna wasn't paying any attention. "I'll talk to Daddy right away. We can have the money ready by this afternoon."

"Come on, Donna, that's enough."

"How much do you think they'll want? Ten thousand? Twenty?"

"Will you stop this?"

Donna looked at her with contempt. "If you won't do this, I'll find someone who will. Or I'll do it myself. Don't you understand?"

It was clear that she meant it. Her face, a moment ago so drawn and weary, now glowed with an almost religious fervor. She was ready to do anything for Marita. She was probably too used to relying on money to take care of problems, Helen realized, and couldn't see beyond her checkbook now.

An hour later Helen was alone again. The two women had argued for a while, but it ended with Donna going to her bank to make arrangements for a large withdrawal of cash right away. Helen rummaged in her desk and dug out the address book she'd started using during her last two years as a cop. There was a number written on the back page. She hadn't used it for a long time, but as she dialed it now her fingers seemed to know it by heart.

Chapter 14

The voice on the other end of the line started out deep and raspy. "Yeah, who is it?"

"Fred? It's Helen Black."

"Fuck." There was a long and heavy sigh. "What the hell you doin' callin' me up like this? I thought you quit, anyway."

"I did, Fred. This is strictly unofficial."

"The hell it is, bitch. You got any idea what will happen if they know I talked to you? I am screwed." His voice was dropping to a whisper, tinged with panic, over the music in the background.

"Did I ever fuck you over, Fred? Come on, haven't I always been straight with you?"

He snorted. "I guess about as straight as a dyke could be. Well. You gonna tell me what you want?"

"I want to know about Danny James, Fred. Who can I talk to?"

"You're crazy, you know that?"

"Freddy, do you want me to go over how many times I saved your hairy old ass? And what I could still do to you if I wanted? You want that, Freddy?"

"Shit." He sighed again, and Helen could almost hear him rub his hand over his face in the familiar gesture he always made. "Look, your old pals have been out here, day and night. Oakland looks like some fuckin' parade, since they found Danny in that vault. I don't need it, you don't need it. Okay?"

"Fred, listen. I'm not working with them. All I want is to talk to somebody. I don't think it had anything to do with you or your, ah, associates. But I have to know more about him. If I could get the people who did this, then the heat would come off and it would be business as usual, right? Fred?"

"And what makes you think they trust me?"

"You're still alive."

She waited through his silence, then heard him laugh. "I must be the crazy one. All right, I ain't gonna promise nothin', you hear me? Nothin'. Give me a call back at three o'clock today. But don't expect a damn thing."

"Fair enough." He hung up, and Helen sat at the desk for a few minutes, trying to still the voices that told her she shouldn't do this. How could she say it would be "business as usual" to someone who ran errands for dealers in Oakland? As a cop, Helen had seen working with informants as a necessary evil. It was just part of the job. She had used Fred a lot in the past, and he had always been a reliable source of information. Somehow, the idea of doing a little business with him now disgusted Helen. The gray areas, the sticky issues had started making her a lot more uncomfortable since she'd opened the agency. Quick utilitarian judgments were no longer possible for her. The realization that she had perhaps been hiding behind a badge and a manual was upsetting enough to get her out of the office and back home to prepare for Danny James' funeral.

Looking at herself in the mirror after she'd showered and dressed, Helen was vividly reminded of the first funeral she'd ever attended. Not Aunt Josephine's, but her grandmother's. Cancer had taken a long time with Grandma Hodges, a slow gnawing rather than ferocious devouring. Her parents hadn't shared the popular belief that children should be kept away from death. Helen had been held up to kiss her grandmother's face before the lid was nailed shut and the coffin lowered into the ground.

The cemetery in Mississippi was a far cry from Hopkins Memorial Gardens. Set in northern Berkeley, on the other side of the campus, it reminded Helen of a trip she'd made to Los Angeles, where she'd been forced to tour a famous cemetery for Hollywood stars. Even then, so many years ago, Helen had been disgusted with the vulgar, simpering angels and the piped organ music. The only thing considered bad taste there was death itself. To cover up everyone's embarrassment at the awful insult, a funeral held at the Hollywood cemetery would be designed as just another movie, served up with glitz and plaster.

Heart-rending wails and a simple pine box were preferable, Helen decided. She wondered what sort of arrangements the James family had made. Maybe Danny's parents hoped that this final show of spurious affection would erase their own guilt and shame about their son.

When she finally located the party, she immediately saw a couple that could only be Mr. and Mrs. James. He was a small, dapper man, wearing a cheap cloth raincoat over his painfully new black suit. On his arm he supported his wife, who looked as though she were still in shock. Her makeup was applied awkwardly, with mascara thickly trailing over her papery eyelids. She teetered on heels that weren't meant to be worn on this soggy ground, and she kept dabbing absently at the tears that flowed noiselessly and ceaselessly down her cheeks. It was an ugly sight, and Helen looked away from them and fixed her eyes on the coffin. Why hadn't they chosen cremation? she wondered angrily. She knew only too well what happened to a victim's remains in an autopsy: the bad jokes about going to lunch, the careless treatment of intimate anatomy that came with the medical examiner's professional ease. The soothing tone of the minister caught her attention and she gave in to it gladly. No matter that the service was being spoken by a complete stranger to the family. The words themselves seemed enough.

It was over, and the tiny group began to move. Helen had stood apart, a little to the side. Watching them now, she saw a telltale overcoat appear behind Mr. and Mrs. James. Lieutenant Haskell had always worn that coat — it was the nearest thing to a trenchcoat he could achieve, and the homicide unit had a perennial joke about it. Their eyes met for a moment, then he melted into the gray tombstones surrounding them. Helen watched him go, then was startled to see Lucille Ogden walking slowly away from the graveside.

Screw Haskell, Helen thought. She had to try to talk to Lucille. Stepping through the tall wet grass she caught up to her. "Mrs. Ogden? May I talk to you?"

"Who is that?"

"My name is Helen Black. We spoke together last night, at the Chamber of Commerce party."

Lucille was astonished. "I had no idea you knew him, too."

Helen did not answer immediately. Instead she took the woman's arm and gently steered her through the graves to the street, feeling Haskell's eyes on both of them. "It's very cold out here. Why don't you let me buy you a cup of coffee?" The woman went obediently, like a child. It wasn't until Helen was starting the engine and asking if Lucille had to be back at the bank that she caved in. Helen turned the motor off and waited for the first flood of weeping to subside.

"I'm so sorry," Lucille whispered, her breath coming more evenly.

"Don't be. Here, I have some more tissues."

"I called in sick today." Lucille wiped her face, and her makeup disappeared, first from one eye, then from the other. "God, I've needed to do that. Don't worry, it won't happen again."

"How about that coffee now?"

Lucille turned and looked at her appraisingly. "You never said what you were doing there today. Who are you?"

"I'm a private detective, Mrs. Ogden."

The information did not distress her. "I thought maybe you were with the police, the way you studied us last night at the party." She stared out the steamed car window. "I know a place we can go. It's only a block away."

Helen obeyed, not wanting to say anything that would make her change her mind. At least the diner Lucille led them to was clean and quiet. Waiting until they had steaming mugs set before them in the booth, Helen said, "Thank you. I've been wanting to talk to someone who really knew him."

"I'm not sure that I did, really," Lucille answered. "Not the important things — not what made him do what he did. And not who killed him. It wasn't me, by the way," she said, looking up from the table. Suddenly Lucille laughed, an odd hysterical noise. "His parents came up to me in the chapel today, wanting to know who I was. It all felt so strange, so — I don't know — surreal. I almost told them. They even invited me to visit them this week at their hotel. They didn't know him any better than I did. But that's probably the way he wanted it. He never let anyone close."

"You first met him at the bank, didn't you?" Helen asked.

Lucille smiled wryly. "I knew they'd find out about that sooner or later. I really think Jerry had totally forgotten about it. Danny just did a little filing, answered phones, things like that. Nothing very important. I doubt if it's related to his death."

"Who do you think killed him?"

She shrugged. "I have no idea. Maybe the police are right, maybe it had to do with drugs. He never talked to me about that."

"So you were close friends?"

"Oh, I thought you already knew. I mean, I thought the police knew. We were lovers."

Helen tried to hide her surprise and began to stir her coffee.

"Not for some time, you know," Lucille went on. "Not since ten years ago."

Ten years ago. Apparently time had done very little to alter Lucille's feelings. "That was when you were working together?" Helen asked.

"Yes, that's when it started. It only lasted a few months. He found someone younger and prettier, I guess. But I always knew that would happen."

Helen decided she must have been starved to talk about it to someone, to anyone. There was no reluctance, no hurt, in Lucille's voice. "What was he like, Mrs. Ogden?"

Lucille smiled, sadly this time. "Sort of unreal, somehow. Like something in a dream. He could make you do wild things, dream wild things along with him. Money, fame, power — he talked about them all the time. As if he could make things real by talking about them." She saw Helen's face and shook her head. "I know you don't understand. It sounds ridiculous to you, but it was what I needed then. What I still need. You see, my husband and I — well, there's nothing there. There hasn't been for years, not since my second daughter was born."

"Did you keep in touch with him after it was over?"

"No, not at all. I was amazed when he walked into the bank a couple of months ago. I think he was, too. He never expected to see me again, I'm sure. I suppose," she added, almost chuckling, "he was afraid I'd say or do something embarrassing, but he didn't have to worry. I wouldn't have done anything to hurt him."

Helen felt appalled at the enormity of the woman's devotion. They sat in silence for a while, then Helen asked, "Do you know of anything that happened back then that might be connected to his death?"

Completely calm now, Lucille shook her head. "It was odd, though, both Jerry and I being assigned to the same branch again. People in the bank transfer around a lot, and their paths don't usually cross. Then Danny started showing up, and suddenly all those memories came back again."

Lucille set her cup down carefully and spoke in a low voice without meeting Helen's gaze. "I know what you're thinking — you want me to tell you that Danny and I were doing something dishonest with the bank back then. But it just isn't true. Maybe he hoped I would, maybe that's why he was interested in me in the first place. And God knows I have my faults. But stealing from the bank isn't one of them."

She looked up with dignity in her eyes and Helen felt a little ashamed. Lucille went on in a shaky voice.

"My job is all I have left now, with the kids gone. My husband couldn't care less about me, and I'm getting old. So I'm not about to do anything to mess up my career."

Helen was on the verge of reaching out to her in

sympathy, her hand lifting up from the table, when Lucille said, "I think I'd like to go back to the cemetery for a while. Alone. Would you please drop me off there?"

So they went back in the persistent fog that kept trying to rain. Neither one of them said a word during the brief journey. Helen knew, as she watched Lucille stepping through the grass to the grave that she was saying goodbye to a great deal more than a dead lover.

Chapter 15

At four o'clock Helen was driving through downtown Oakland in the direction of the pier. The fog had never really lifted, and it was nearly dark. There was quite a lot of work being done on Broadway lately, and motorists were tentatively inching through a maze of orange cones, peering over their steering wheels in anxiety. At last the narrow lanes eased back into their normal patterns once she passed the signs indicating she was near the airport. She continued slowly, going under an overpass, realizing her unfamiliarity with this part of town. There it was — a sign crossed her line of vision — Second Street. She turned right.

Here there were large warehouses and import stores, some open to the public and displaying their goods in stalls on the sidewalks. The bright colors and interesting objects spread out for the perusal of last-minute holiday shoppers lent an air of festivity to the drab buildings and alleys — an air that would, she knew, dissipate quickly when darkness fell. She parked on a side street just past the warehouse section and walked back to the hamburger place on Second. Fred's last warning to her went through her mind as she walked.

"Now look, this man is not going to be jerked around, you understand me? He thinks you half crazy for doin' something like this. And if he sees any of your little friends around, we can both kiss our ass goodbye, you hear me?"

No one in the restaurant noticed her as she entered. The room was amazingly small and crowded. Shoppers impatient to get back to the sales were grabbing their greasy dinners and soft drinks and fighting their way back outside. Dazed by the noise and confusion and the smell of frying, Helen stood still just inside the door. Then she saw them.

One man was perched on a stool at the counter next to the wall opposite the door. A burning cigarette in one hand, he held a styrofoam cup of coffee in the other. Another man was in a corner a few feet away from her, munching french fries and seemingly almost asleep, with heavy-lidded eyes fixed dreamily on the door behind her. Two men sat at a

117

table in the farthest corner. As she stood there, one of these men got up and walked over, grinning broadly.

A tall, skinny young man, his grin was maniacally boyish, and she suspected his coke habit was quite expensive. He bubbled over with amusement at some private joke. "Won't you join us?" he asked, and Helen followed his black-clad back to the table and sat down. A hamburger and french fries appeared on a thick paper plate before her.

"We weren't sure what you wanted to drink," the other man said in a slow drawl. His voice and manner were a foil for the ill-concealed frenzy of his companion.

"Iced tea would be fine, thanks." She spoke to the skinny youth, who scurried over to the cashier.

"I know this place looks like shit, but he makes a pretty good hamburger. Try it." There was nothing but polite interest in his gaze, so Helen obligingly bit into his offering and looked up in surprise. "Told you," he laughed.

Helen studied him as she took another bite. It was difficult to guess at his parentage. That dark skin and the round dark eyes, a soft brown, could have been a result of any number of mixtures. She was struck by his incredible good looks. He had a nascent, languorous strength, tinged with cruelty, that probably served him well as an aphrodisiac for women looking for danger.

"Freddy tells me you want to discuss a mutual acquaintance."

She nodded and put her hamburger down. "Yes. I appreciate your taking the time out to talk to me."

His businesslike tone was contagious. "I don't know what Freddy told you about me."

He regarded her for a long moment in which she feared that the whole thing was off. Then he threw back his head and laughed again. The boy sitting with them jumped.

"That Fred! He's an asshole but he's honest. I can always count on him 'cause he's too dumb to lie and mean it." Realizing that somehow she'd passed an esoteric test, Helen took a long drink from her tea.

Suddenly the man stood up. "Excuse me," he said with a deep mock bow, and he went to say something to the man who sat by the door. When he returned, Helen got up.

"I think we'll go outside now. Take care of it." This last remark was made to the boy, who hopped over to the cash register to settle the bill. Helen left with her host, the other two men following at a distance.

It was almost completely dark now, but the sales were still going strong. "I like crowds," he said. "I like to see people enjoying themselves. Makes me feel good." He had put on a leather jacket and gloves and spoke without looking at her. "Best place in the world to carry on a private conversation is in a crowd of strangers."

They continued walking. He paused once or twice to look at some of the imported wares spread out on the table in front of him. "Danny James was a real fuckhead," he said musingly as he examined a delicate basket, turning it around in his large hands. "I allowed him to do a little business in my area. For the proper fee, of course. He wanted to break out on his own, keep going east into Contra Costa County." They moved out of an eager group of bargain hunters. "Said that's where the future was, all the little yuppies in their houses on the hill. Sounded like a fuckin' realtor tryin' to sell me a patch of weeds in Grass Valley."

Helen had to smile at the comparison. She asked, "Did you ever see his operation as being important? Did it look like it might turn into something big?"

He shrugged. "Looked half-assed to me. But I admit that the whole thing about this business is you gotta have an open mind. You gotta be ready to change or do something new. You see, people like it, if it's new. That's half the fun for them." He was now crossing a street and Helen felt rather than saw the bodyguards behind them.

"Did he ever mention the bank to you? Maybe some job he was planning for the bank was a part of the operation."

"Hell, the little ratfucker was always shooting off his mouth. I never paid too much attention to it. The last time I saw him he was going on about pulling off a big thing somewhere, but he didn't say it was at the bank. Just told me to wait and see, he was going to prove he was a big, bad sonofabitch."

"How long ago was that?"

"Two weeks, maybe three." The same time Danny had visited Andre Spicer.

"Poor little motherfucker," he was saying. "He was stupid, and that's the biggest mistake you can make. You're not interested enough in the operation, I used to tell him. Too hung up on showing off. And that's what killed him, I guarantee it. But I don't want to speak ill of the dead."

He had stopped abruptly. Helen saw that they'd walked behind one of the warehouses. There were people on the other side, of course, but they probably wouldn't hear anything that went on back here. Idiot, she cursed herself, feeling her anger and fear at the same time. The two bodyguards were standing at either end of the building, and the skinny child had appeared out of nowhere to perch behind her, breathing heavily. She could feel his breath, smell his sweat.

"I hear you like pussy."

Was it a threat? A taunt? "Yes. I'm a lesbian."

"Not bad for a dyke. Not bad at all." The soft brown eyes roamed over her body, weighing and measuring. "I like pussy, too."

She turned and willed herself to walk away slowly. "Hope you enjoyed the hamburger!" he called out after her, and she heard him laugh one more time.

Helen hardly knew how she got to a pay phone after that. With fingers just beginning to tremble she dialed her ex-partner's number. At the last minute, she'd asked Manny to hang around and wait for her call, just as they used to do when they were partners. She could remember only too well the way she used to feel, staying late, grabbing the telephone the instant the first ring sounded.

Manny answered before the second ring. "Jesus Christ! I don't ever want you to do a thing like that again. Stupid, stupid! And I was stupid to let you do it. Do you realize it's five-fifteen! Fifteen minutes after you were supposed to check in." In his own fear he sounded enraged, but the sharp words were welcome to Helen.

"Okay, Manny, you can shut up now. You don't have to worry, I am never going to repeat this experience."

"If you do, I promise to kill you before they do. Go home."

Helen hung up and shakily drove back to Berkeley.

Chapter 16

Frieda turned over in bed. It was dark. Helen couldn't see her expression, but her tone of voice spoke volumes.

"Christ, Helen. You could have been killed. What the hell made you do it?"

Once again Helen sighed and cursed herself for having had those two shots of whiskey before Frieda arrived. As soon as she'd stepped inside the door after getting back from Oakland, she'd headed for the cabinet where she kept liquor. It was an attempt to calm down, to still the shaking that had overwhelmed her on the way home. A mistake, as usual. It made Helen want to pour the whole thing out, seeking comfort in her lover's arms. She generally avoided drinking precisely because it left her bereft of defenses. Loss of control terrified her.

At first Frieda had been frightened for her, concerned and consoling. But the first shock had worn off as the night progressed, and they'd ended up in the bedroom. They'd started out clasped in each others' arms, but as the conversation continued in the dark their bodies had separated, each drifting towards the edge of the bed. Frieda lay flat and rigid under the sheets.

"Where the hell does she get off asking you to wander around Oakland with a drug dealer and ask questions about another dealer who's turned up dead? My God, I just can't believe you'd even think of it!"

"Look, Frieda, if I hadn't, she was good and ready to go herself. I couldn't let her do that. At least I'm used to talking to these kinds of people. It wasn't quite the same as her going to meet him."

Frieda moved abruptly and propped herself on her elbow. One hand reached behind her to switch on a lamp, and Helen blinked in the sudden brightness. Frieda's face was flushed and stern. "Are you sure that was it?" she asked. "Or are you still trying to prove something?"

It was the same old argument. Helen felt drained of everything, every emotion, even anger. "I don't know what you're talking about."

Frieda shook her head. Helen watched her long hair swaying in the soft light of the lamp. "Oh, yes, you do, Helen. You always have to be tough, hard as nails, cold as ice, all the clichés. A big, bad dyke. It's

124

been this way since day one, when you were with the police and now with this agency of yours."

At the mention of the agency Helen began to lose her temper. "I'm not trying to prove anything, Frieda," she said angrily. "I'm just trying to do a good job for my client. And to make something out of this case for the agency."

But Frieda ignored her response. "You do it with me, too," she went on as she lay down again. "This detective stuff is taking you away from me, even worse than before. All you think about now is solving problems, solving people as if they were problems. What do I have to do, get involved in a crime before you notice me?"

The effect of the whiskey or her unaccustomed, nearly empty stomach was having a belated effect on her. Helen felt a little dizzy, yet oddly wide awake. She lay very still, staring at the ceiling, and let Frieda's frustration flow over the bed.

"You couldn't take a few minutes out of your time to see the exhibit yesterday, and you knew how important it was to me."

"Frieda, please! I'm really sorry about that, but you have to understand —"

"Oh, I see. I have to understand. Why is it that it's always me that has to understand everything? Why don't you try understanding me for a change?"

"All right, Frieda," Helen sighed, rubbing a hand over her forehead. "All right. You tell me what to understand. At the moment, what I understand is that it sounds like you've had enough of me and this relationship. That seems clear. But I don't understand why you keep coming back, if that's how you feel." This is it, Helen thought. She forced herself to keep her face and voice calm and prepared to face the truth.

"Oh, God, Helen," Frieda said through tears. "I don't know why I do this. I'm not even angry, really. I just feel so afraid."

"Afraid of what?"

"You don't know —" She broke off, fighting back tears. "You just don't know what it was like when you were a cop. I couldn't stand it, some nights, waiting for you to call. Especially when we'd planned for something and you didn't show up. Why do you think I hesitated so much about moving in with you? Every night you were late or didn't call I was so scared something had happened to you!"

"Frieda, you never said anything." Helen reached out to her, groping for her hand. "Frieda —"

"I never said anything because I know how it upsets you to confront feelings. Mine or yours. I've always tried to let you have that distance since you seemed to need it so much." Frieda was calmer now. Her hand held Helen's tightly. "Now that we share a house, and share our lives, that makes it even worse. If something were to happen to you now, this place would be full of ghosts. Your clothes, your books, the furniture, every room. Even," she added with a trace of a smile, "even the cat."

"You make it sound like I'm training to be a kamikaze pilot," Helen said, trying to encourage the dim glimmer of humor.

"Well, you won't exactly be a den mother for the Cub Scouts, either."

They shifted a little in the bed, moving closer. Helen decided it was safe enough to risk a question.

"You still haven't told me why you stay."

126

"You can't figure it out?" Frieda was suddenly on top of her, her face close, her breath warm. "You're a regular femme fatale, Helen. A belle dame sans merci." Her breasts rested on Helen's, caressing them with their soft weight, arousing flickers of warmth that rippled into waves of warmth that rippled into waves of heat.

It was Frieda who always approached Helen, Frieda who broke the tension and crossed the distance. Helen could wait, wanting her, aching for her, hoping she would do the reaching and save her from exposing her own need. But now, tonight, Helen wanted it to be different. She couldn't stop the low moan in her throat as she lifted her hands to stroke Frieda's shoulders. "I have no pale warriors on the hillside, Frieda," she whispered. "Only you. Don't you know that by now?"

"Yes. Yes, I do know it." Her mouth found Helen's and they didn't need words. Helen pulled her down, feeling the whole weight of her, the length of her, covering her body. Frieda kissed her again, insistent, demanding response. Helen slid her hands down from Frieda's shoulders to her hips. Frieda's body was slim, contrasting sharply with her own solid separateness. The difference always excited Helen, and she held Frieda even more tightly.

"I want you so badly, all the time," Frieda said. "After all this time, all these years, that hasn't changed."

Helen grasped her hips and they began to move together. If Frieda was surprised at the way Helen was taking charge, she didn't show it. She flung her hair back as she moved in rhythm with Helen, her head tilted back, her eyes closed. "Yes, yes," she breathed. She moved faster and faster until her body shuddered with pleasure and she gasped, her orgasm flowing onto them both.

It wasn't enough for Helen. Gently she rose and made Frieda lie down. Moving slowly, she laved Frieda's body with her tongue, lingering on all the spots she knew were most sensitive. Finally she reached her thighs. Stroking them apart, Helen's fingers and tongue found the soft sweetness that was hidden there. She felt the muscles tighten and release over and over, gathering with greater intensity every time she moved inside her. Frieda's sharp intake of breath, her cries — they spurred Helen on to probe deeper. This time her climax was longer. With one brief, sharp cry she arched her back and clutched at the sheets. "Oh, Helen," she murmured, "I love you so much, so much."

Helen moved back up next to her and held her close, her fingertips tracing Frieda's spine, picking up the film of sweat. "Frieda, what happens? Why do we get into the same old arguments?"

Frieda chuckled, a drowsy noise. "I can tell you why. We're scared to death of each other, Helen. I'm terrified I'll lose you to some thug and you're afraid you might actually need me in your life. Or that I'll find out you do."

Helen cradled her lover's head on her breast. Frieda spoke without rancor, simply accepting the fact of their relationship. Helen wondered, not for the first time, why she found it so hard to relax and enjoy what they had together. Years ago Helen had learned the lessons of loneliness — that the best way to avoid pain was simply not to feel. Not even for Frieda, it seemed could she let go of that conviction.

It was too easy to blame her childhood, spent in the poorest section of the South, for her fears, but Helen knew that it was not the complete answer.

"Hey, where did you go?" Frieda asked.

"Sorry, I was just thinking."

"What about?"

"About you."

"Well, that's encouraging. Do I get to hear about it?"

Helen held her closer and smiled. "Just admiring you for being able to put up with me."

"Like I keep telling you — you're quite a challenge."

"I wish I weren't."

"It's okay, Helen." Frieda kissed her throat and nestled down in the sheets, making a warm nest for herself as she always did. Helen, too, felt relaxed and sleepy for the first time in days. Tired of her own restless thoughts, she deliberately put them out of her mind. Only Frieda's skin, her hair, her scent — these found their way into her sense and overpowered her consciousness, lulling her to sleep.

Chapter 17

Jerry Neely turned the pages of the final audit report and tried to follow what Ed Grant was saying. Jerry reached for his cup of coffee and sipped. Damn! It had grown cold. The cream had congealed on the surface and left a greasy film around the rim of the cup. Concealing a small shudder of distaste, he set the cup back down and looked at the file in front of him on the polished table.

He took a quick glance at Ed. The man hadn't touched his coffee. It was probably cold by now, too.

Ed was looking down, reading in his clear, precise voice, the voice that drove Jerry crazy with its finicky pronunciation. He'd tried for years to like Ed Grant, but he had never been able to get over his revulsion. The sight of the pale auditor, smoothing down his thick white hair and calmly turning the pages of the report, filled him with a mixture of panic and irritation. Jerry wanted nothing more than to throw the cold coffee at the man sitting opposite, bathing both him and the damning report he was reading in pale brown liquid.

And the report was damning. It came down hard on the branch performance during the past year. "You'll note," Ed droned on, "in going through the books I found several reports filed out of date order. There were also two instances of totals in the cash account which were not immediately cleared."

Jerry started to protest, but stopped when he saw it would be no use. They were going to get a three rating this year, three instead of the hoped for four. That's what the Berkeley office had received last year. It's better than going down to a two, Jerry told himself, but he knew that the regional office would look with disfavor on any branch that did not improve from a mere average rating. Promotions and raises could be affected, not just for him but for Lucille as well. Feeling the need to do something, anything, to relieve his tension, Jerry pressed the buzzer on the desk behind him. Ed looked up over his rimless spectacles, surprised.

"Just a second, Ed," Jerry said, belatedly. Lorie's voice sounded over the intercom, fuzzy and bored.

"Would you bring us in some more coffee, Lorie?"

"I'll have to make a fresh pot," she responded, clearly peeved at being disturbed for such a petty reason.

"If you don't mind." Jerry released the button and turned back to Ed. They were sitting in the conference room, a tiny glassed-in space that afforded some privacy, encased in thick curtains. Employees were brought here for counseling or reprimands; annual performance evaluations were conducted here; customers with embarrassing or awkward problems would be shown in to this room for an interview. Jerry had always liked the little pocket of peace in this office, but now it made him feel claustrophobic, as if he were penned in by some predator.

Ed resumed his monologue. "So, as you can see, Jerry, I have no other choice but to give you a three rating. I'm sorry I can't give you any better. There's been no noticeable improvement since last year."

Jerry squirmed and tried to keep the pleading tone out of his voice as he answered. "Actually, Ed, I didn't see anything about our, uh, our four robberies during the year. You remember those? Two of them with armed robbers, shotguns, no less. And the employee turnover has been pretty heavy. We've had three new people to bring in and take time to train. I didn't see anything about that in your report. Not to mention the stress we've all been under since last week. You know that doesn't make for stability in a branch." Jerry knew his face must be red and he cleared his throat a couple of times. Where the hell was that girl with the coffee? He needed something to occupy his hands. Right now they were shuffling the pages of the report, fumbling about stupidly. He grabbed his pen and began to drum it on the table.

Ed was putting the report back into its folder. He didn't look up at Jerry. "My job is to report on branch activity reflected by the findings of the audit. Any extenuating circumstances should be discussed with regional headquarters, not me. You know the procedures."

Ed had packed his briefcase, snapped it shut, and now turned around to pick up his coat. He was still using that dingy parka that seemed so out of place with his customary natty appearance. Somehow the sight of that parka encouraged Jerry to do something he would later regret as an idiotic act born of desperation. He was just another guy, Jerry prodded himself. Maybe he would listen to reason. Maybe talking about the old days, how they all used to stick together, would help Ed to be a little easier on them in his report.

Jerry launched into a rambling speech, stuffing as much bonhomie into it as he could manage. It worked on many of the customers he'd talked to. Why not with old Ed Grant, whom Jerry had known for years? The good ol' boy network that Jerry was used to working with would respond favorably to his technique of back-slapping and hand-pumping. "After all, Ed," he said, "we've known each other for a long time. You know I'm good with the customers. That's the bottom line, isn't it? How you deal with the public. Why, I got a whole bunch of letters sent to headquarters last year, letters from customers, telling those folks at the regional office how happy they were banking here. Wait just a sec, I got copies of 'em here — no, I think they're in this drawer —"

He finally found them buried deep in the desk. Ed was unimpressed with the offering. He even looked embarrassed. "If head office had copies of those letters, then it's up to them to decide how to use them. I have no control over that." His look of disgust went straight to the older man's heart like a knife.

"Come on now, Ed," Jerry whined. "What do you want to be such a hardass for? Why don't you ease up a bit?"

"I'm merely doing my job, Jerry. It's not a question of friendship —"

"The hell it ain't! All us guys that started out with the bank back in the sixties, why, we were a team, Ed. We believed in looking out for each other. You used to believe in it, too."

But Ed's face remained frozen. "Please, Jerry. You're putting me in a very awkward position by saying all this. We can't bring personal issues into it."

Jerry watched him put on the parka over the pin-stripe suit, grasp the leather briefcase and turn to go. This was it, his last chance. Looking back on it, Jerry could only kick himself for being such a fool for what he said next.

"Look here, Ed. Just because you're having a hard time right now —"

"What on earth are you talking about?" The auditor stood still and his pale eyes narrowed.

"Hell, we all know you don't have it too easy at home these days. I mean, what with Gladys and all. But good God, man, that's no reason to be taking

things out on the people you work with, you know?"
He got up and gestured as if to pat Ed on the back,
man to man.

The look on Ed's face stopped him. He was always
pale and cold-looking, but now the auditor was
positively icy. The gray eyes hardened into flint, and
his voice came out like a recording, carefully
controlled.

"I don't know what the hell you're trying to say,
Jerry, but I suggest you stop right there. If you want
to get personal now, let me just remind you of the
fact that you're the one who hired Danny James ten
years ago. I bet you thought everyone had forgotten
about that, didn't you?"

Jerry ran a pudgy hand over his sweating
forehead. "That was such a long time ago, Ed. It has
nothing to do with what happened here last week."

"Oh, no? What about this Spicer girl? Marita?
You hired her, too. Frankly, I don't think the bank
wants that kind of person for an employee." Ed was
leaning over the table now, almost breathing in
Jerry's face. The look of disgust had returned to his
face, and Jerry instinctively leaned back in his chair,
away from the other man.

"Now there's no way I could have known
anything about this James bastard when I hired him,
was there? And I don't know what you mean about
Marita. She's a good employee." Jerry was sweating
and his voice shook.

Satisfied at seeing Jerry cower, Ed stood up
straight. "I don't know, Jerry. Headquarters might
see it differently. Seems to me I recall how you closed
your eyes to a few things going on in the wire
transfer department while James was working there."

"You son of a bitch," Jerry sputtered. "What the hell is it that you get off on, making people miserable?"

But Ed ignored him, too angry to let it go. "Anyone who would hire a girl who goes out to dinner with scum like Danny James is going to have some serious explaining to do."

"You mean Marita?" Jerry asked, incredulous. "But she's really a nice gal. You gonna pick on her, now?"

Ed shook his head and reached again for his parka and briefcase. "You're missing the point again. I'm not here to pick on anybody, just to do a necessary job. A job that helps keep Greater East Bay Bank going. You need to grow up and realize that fact, Jerry. Quit trying to use that teamwork shit with me."

With this he stomped out of the room, nearly running over Lorie in the process. She had come up behind him quietly, bearing a tray with a carafe of fresh coffee and two clean cups. Her entrance had been so unobtrusive, so unlike her usual manner, that neither of them had noticed her. How long has she been standing there? Jerry wondered miserably. And just how much of that lovely little scene did she witness? The auditor edged his way past her through the door and was gone. Lorie stood gazing at Mr. Neely, still holding the tray, her face a beautiful blank above her red silk dress.

"Just set it down, Lorie," Jerry said, almost snapping at her. She obeyed, her eyes bright and full of excitement. He turned his back to her to pour himself a cup of coffee so that she wouldn't see his hands trembling. God, wouldn't she ever leave?

"Did you need anything else, Mr. Neely?" she asked in her innocent high-pitched voice.

"No, Lorie, no thanks." He swiveled around in his chair. "Oh, I nearly forgot. Did you ever get a chance to call up Ted with those figures for the loan? Better do that before eleven. He won't be in his office this afternoon." She flounced out of the room and shut the door behind her.

Finally Jerry was alone. He set the cup, steaming and fragrant, down on the table before him. A bottle of whiskey, half-full, winked at him from behind some files. Jerry knew he could be fired for having alcohol on the premises, but it was another risk he'd always been willing to take. As he added a little to his coffee, a fleeting thought of Bob Scanlon passed through his mind. When the police had examined the security guard's body, they'd found a small flask of whiskey in one of his pockets. Hard to blame the guy. It must have been very cold and lonely here, night after night, with no one to talk to. Jerry took a sip of the doctored coffee and felt the whiskey hit his nerves. They needed strengthening. "Fuck you, Greater East Bay Bank," he muttered as he unscrewed the cap again. "Fuck you, Ed Grant. Fuck 'em all."

* * * * *

Sitting at her huge uncluttered desk, Lorie heard the scrape of the drawer in Mr. Neely's office. She knew what it was. Everyone in the branch knew about the whiskey. That wasn't what she was thinking about right now, anyway. She had other, more interesting things on her mind. With quick steps she went across the lobby to Mattie's teller window and began to whisper to her.

Evelyn saw them talking and shook her head. "Look at those two again," she said to Marita, who was counting a cash shipment with her. "Just like back in grade school."

Marita smiled. Things had been going better lately. Donna was still hanging around a lot, but she couldn't really complain about that. After all, she just wanted to make sure her prize possession was safe. It didn't hurt to go along with it for the ride. Then there was Helen Black. Marita found the detective strangely attractive. It was odd. Helen wasn't beautiful. She was hardly even friendly. Maybe it was just that she seemed so strong, so steady. Like a rock. Solid as a rock.

"What on earth —" Evelyn was staring at the front door, her eyes huge with surprise behind the thick lenses of her glasses. Marita turned to look. Someone had walked into the bank, shouting, "All right, everybody! This is a stickup!" He pointed clasped hands out in front of him and swung around, stiff-armed, in a parody of a robber pointing a gun and sweeping the room with it. Then he relaxed and began to laugh hysterically. Jerry Neely came out of his office to see what was going on.

"Just kidding, just kidding, folks. See? Look, ma, no guns!" He held his hands out and kept laughing until his eyes streamed with tears, his body doubling over in hilarity.

"Terrific. Just what we need after everything else that's happened." Marita hardly heard Evelyn's comment. She was too stunned to respond. The man was her brother Andre.

Chapter 18

Marita felt dizzy for a moment. In the trauma of the last few days, she had almost managed to forget about him. He loomed in front of her now like a ghost, looking a little cleaner and better dressed than when she'd last seen him, but still with the same slightly manic glow to his face. Coke again, she thought despairingly.

"How's the kid doin'? Hanging in there?"

"I'm fine, Andre, but I have to work now," she said in a voice that hardly trembled at all. It was no use. Evelyn stood, curious and smiling at her teller window, waiting for an introduction. "This is my brother, Andre."

"How are you?" Evelyn greeted him innocently. "Are you in town for the holidays?"

"Uh, yeah, yeah, that's it. Thought I'd look up my little baby sister, take her out to lunch, you know," he rambled. His attention was caught by the Christmas tree, then by the pretty young girl sitting in front of it. A slow grin moved across his mouth.

"I don't know when I'll be going to lunch, Andre," Marita told him. "You should have called me first."

"Huh? Oh, well, I just wanted to give you a surprise, you know?"

By now Lucille had seen them talking. "Who's that?" Andre wanted to know, feeling her censorious gaze.

"That's my supervisor, Lucille. I really shouldn't be talking to you, Andre, there are customers waiting in line."

"You mean to tell me you don't have time for your big brother? The one who sent you to school all those years? When you got kicked out in the cold?"

Customers and staff alike were watching with interest now, although Andre spoke only for her to hear. Marita tried to control the dismay she knew her face revealed and went to check the lunch schedule hanging on the wall behind Lucille's desk. Her hopes for a late lunch period were dashed immediately. Upon finding out who the man at her window was, Lucille couldn't have been more accommodating.

"We'll switch you with Mattie, so you can go early. How about eleven-thirty? You'll avoid the crowds that way."

141

For just a moment Marita wished that she could tell Lucille everything — all the things she could never tell Donna, or Helen, or Andre. She'd noticed Lucille sometimes. The older woman was suffering something, Marita was sure of that. Would she understand the passionate desire to run from everything, to disappear without a trace from the people, the questions? But she felt Lucille staring at her and the moment passed. Better get it over with.

Andre was waiting for her in one of the high-backed armchairs by the front door, placed there for the convenience of customers compelled to wait for service. He looked around him with an air of amusement, inspecting the periodicals and newsletters displayed on the polished tables with a studied mockery, drawing attention to himself with his sighs and cluckings. Mr. Neely had emerged from his office and sat at a desk, bent over the audit report. He looked up as Andre flopped about in the chair. After looking pointedly at Andre for about a minute he continued studying the file before him.

"He sure looks a lot like you," Evelyn said to Marita as she locked her cash drawers.

"It's only skin deep," Marita said softly.

"What was that?"

"Nothing." Marita unlocked and passed through the barrier door and approached her brother. Not for the first time, Marita cursed the close proximity they all worked in. No one escaped the eyes of the others, and she sensed Janet's and Lorie's eyes piercing her back. The minute they had gone, she knew, the talk would begin. "I can meet you at the Tacqueria, next to the Claremont Hotel, at eleven-thirty. Wait for me there."

"In other words, get the hell out of here, right?" he giggled. "Okay, okay! I get the message, baby sister. Besides," he added, jerking his head at the corner where Jerry Neely was still reading, "this old fart here don't seem any too pleased 'bout my hangin' around. Who is he, anyway?"

"He's the manager. You probably make him nervous, sitting over here staring at everyone."

Andre got up, still grinning, and walked out. "I'll be waiting for you," he sang over his shoulder as he went through the door. Marita felt angry with herself because she knew her face must be a bright red. She went back to her window and tried to do some work, acutely conscious of the fact that Janet and Lorie were whispering together, with glances turned in her direction. Evelyn, however, avoided meeting Marita's eyes, aware that the girl was upset.

It was just past ten now. On impulse, Marita left her window, picked up a telephone, and dialed the number for Helen's office. She'd memorized it the first night they had talked. Shit — just the answering machine! Marita almost hung up, irritated beyond belief, then decided to go ahead and leave a brief message. Too bad if the others overheard. They'd be talking about it for the rest of the day, anyway.

"This is Marita. I'm calling from work. Andre came in this morning and asked me to meet him for lunch. We'll be at the Tacqueria by the Claremont if you'd like to join us." As she hung up, she had a sudden desire to go to Helen's office. It was somewhere on Shattuck, those new buildings near the University. No, she decided, that would be a stupid idea.

143

The time passed all too quickly, and soon Marita was searching the Tacqueria for her brother. He was sitting at a table at the back of the dining room. There were only two other tables being used, since it was still early. The bar, however, was already full — young men and women who were just beginning to find their alcoholic levels or those who saw no reason to change habits they'd started as high school students. Marita, although she was roughly their age, felt centuries older. Their posturing and pretensions to wisdom only increased the irritation she already felt.

"Why are you so grouchy?" Andre exclaimed as she sat down. "You act like your best friend just died. Maybe he did, huh?"

"Shut up, Andre," she whispered tersely. "You wanted to see me, so here I am, all right?" Marita grabbed the menu from the table and stared at it without seeing what was printed there. A waiter, who recognized Marita from previous visits, came up smiling but she hardly saw him. "A taco salad, please. No, nothing to drink, thanks." When he had gone, she sat back in her chair, arms folded, ready for attack. "Well? I'm waiting."

"You know," Andre said expansively, relaxing into a slump, "this is quite a nice little restaurant, isn't it? The kind they write stuff about in the papers, with little stars and stuff. I ought to do this more often."

"Did you come to the bank and embarrass the hell out of me just to talk about fine dining?"

"Not exactly. Don't rush me, don't rush me. I'm just thinking about how things are going to be changing for me real soon."

144

"What are you talking about?"

"I'm talking about making some money. Lots of it. Enough to take you out to places like this, whenever you want."

Her blood chilled. This could only be bad. "Andre, have you been out on the streets again?"

"Hell, no! It's even better than that!" He was practically jumping in his chair with excitement. "I know a way to get my hands on more than that."

"So what is it?"

He answered her with his mouth full of chips and salsa. "First, you tell me about those people at the bank. The ones you work with."

"Why?"

"Just tell me, okay? Like the broad at the desk, the blonde in the red dress. The one with the tits. I know I seen her somewhere before."

Marita stared. "I'm not telling you a damn thing, Andre. What the hell has gotten into you?"

"You dumb cunt!" he hissed through clenched teeth. "Here I am, tryin' to get us set up for life, and all you can do is sit on your brains."

Maybe it wasn't coke. He'd never been this obnoxious to her before, no matter how high he was. She was beginning to feel fear. "I am walking out of here if you don't calm down. Do you understand me?" Please, Helen, she thought, show up soon.

"Okay. Okay. It's cool, I'm fine, you're fine." He was sweating. "You shouldn't make me mad like that, though."

"All right. You'd better explain —" She stopped and tried to smile as the young waiter placed her taco salad on the table.

"Now, just listen a minute," Andre said. "Who do

you think killed Danny James? The man in the moon, stupid? No, it was one of those people in the bank! Right?" She didn't respond, so he went on. "I am trying to find out who it is, so why don't you just tell me all their names?"

"You really have lost it this time, Andre."

"No, no, see, then I make a little deal with whoever it is. I got an idea which one, anyway."

"What do you mean, a deal?"

"What a moron! A deal, for money. You know — a business proposition, as they say in the movies."

Suddenly it was all so ludicrous: the nervous little waiter, hovering close by, the interested diners, Andre's sweaty, small face luminous in the dim light. She started to laugh helplessly.

"Shut up! Just shut up laughing!"

"Oh, I'm sorry, Andre. It's just that if you knew what the last few days of my life have been like! Forget it." Marita sighed and regarded him ruefully. "Somehow I just can't see you in the role of a blackmailer. Anyway, if you know something you should tell the police."

"Hey, I thought we were family. You know, blood and water and all that shit. You sure didn't mind before when I paid for your tuition."

That stung. "You know damn well I was out of there when I found out where the money came from."

"Fine. Fine," he said, wounded and proud. "One day you'll be sorry." He got up clumsily from the table, catching a corner of the tablecloth on the zipper of his jacket. As he fumbled with it a familiar voice sounded behind him.

146

"Oh, I doubt that." It was Helen. Marita let out a sigh of relief.

Andre sat back down slowly. "What the hell is she doing here?"

Helen sat down and asked the fascinated waiter for a glass of wine. "I know it's a bit early, but I could use one. I'm going to be facing Christmas shopping this afternoon. So, what's the deal, Andre? And who is it with?"

Andre looked from one to the other of them in frustration. Finally he stood up again and backed away from the table. "I don't have to tell you nothin'," he mumbled. He went through the dining room, almost running, disappeared past the bar and out into the street.

Marita closed her eyes and leaned back into her chair. "Thank God you showed up. I hope you don't mind. I just didn't know what else to do."

"What happened?" In the soft lighting of the restaurant, Helen saw that Marita was dressed conservatively again. The woman seemed younger, more vulnerable than ever.

"Honest to God, I don't know what is going on." Marita told her about Andre's swaggering appearance at the bank, the hints, the suggestion of blackmail. "He wouldn't tell me anything after that. Just that he knew something about someone."

Helen frowned. "Did he mention anyone in particular?"

"Well —" She hesitated, "He did ask about Lorie. I won't tell you how he described her."

"I can guess," Helen chuckled. After that, it seemed easier for Marita to tackle the taco salad.

147

Helen ordered fajitas, and soon they were having an amiable lunch together. Marita broke down and allowed herself one glass of wine.

"I really shouldn't," she protested as she took a sip. "I do have to balance tonight, you know."

"You'll be fine," Helen said. The light was directed behind Marita, and the girl's hair looked glossy reflected in its gleam. Her wide dark eyes shone in the flicker of the cheap candle set in a jar on the table as she looked up. Helen's hand was on the table dangerously close to Marita's. Their fingers brushed as they both reached for the bill.

"Please, let me," Helen said, confused.

"No, no, I called you." She allowed Marita to pick up the check, although she knew a bank clerk couldn't make much money. Helen didn't trust herself to say the right thing at the moment.

"You're sure you don't mind that I called you?"

"Not at all. I enjoyed lunch."

"Me, too. Maybe sometime —"

"Yes?" Helen was careful to keep her voice casual.

"Oh, nothing. Thanks. See you later." And she was gone.

Helen followed a few minutes later, unable to keep Marita's almond-shaped eyes from her mind. That's the last time I have a glass of wine in the middle of the day, she told herself.

Chapter 19

During the morning before she met Marita at the restaurant, Helen had phoned the bank. She was immediately put on hold. While waiting Helen was treated to the latest soft-rock hits courtesy of Muzak. Suddenly she heard Lucille's voice.

"This is Lucille Ogden."

"Good morning. This is Helen Black."

There was a long silence on the other end, but Helen had expected that. "This is quite a surprise," Lucille said finally. "I'm sure you didn't call to get information about opening an account."

"I was hoping you would do me a favor."

"That depends. What is it?"

"I'm trying to locate Mr. and Mrs. James. Danny's parents. You told me they'd invited you to visit them at their hotel. I thought you might tell me which hotel that was." Helen didn't relish the idea of spending the entire morning calling all the hotels in the Oakland area.

"And you were sure I'd tell you?"

"No, I wasn't. But I thought you'd like to know who killed him just as much as I do."

"Well, you happen to be wrong about that. It's over and done with now, and I for one don't want to keep thinking about it." Helen waited through another long silence, then Lucille spoke again, very fast. "The Holiday Inn, on Hegenberger Road. Next to the airport." She had hung up before Helen could thank her.

An hour later, just as Marita was introducing Andre to Evelyn, Helen turned off the freeway onto Hegenberger Road. As usual, there was a great deal of traffic. She went back over the phone call she'd made to Mr. and Mrs. James as she drove into the hotel's parking lot. They had been anxious to talk to her, as it turned out. They didn't seem at all interested in the fact that she was a private investigator, and Helen felt they simply wanted to talk to someone, anyone, about their son. Although she'd told them quite honestly what her purpose was, she still was haunted by a vague sense of guilt, as if she'd set up the interview under false pretenses.

Helen waited on a hard orange chair in the drafty lobby after calling their room from the front desk, being observed all the while by the receptionist, a lean woman with a frizzy hairdo peering at her through wire-rimmed glasses. The staff of the hotel had probably figured out who Mr. and Mrs. James were by now, and Helen was sure that her visit to them would be a topic of discussion. It was with relief that she saw the elderly couple get off the elevator and advance uncertainly into the lobby. The closer they came, the more Helen realized that her vision of them as shaken to the core by the violent death of their son had been sentimental and false. They were stunned, perhaps, but far from showing the usual signs of grief.

She rose to greet them, hand outstretched. "Thank you so much for agreeing to see me," she said, as warmly as she could. Mr. James responded with his own hand, trembling slightly. Helen could see now that he was much older than he first appeared, and that he suffered from some form of palsy. His wife took her hand next, hesitating, as if she wasn't used to shaking hands at all. Her skin, which was probably clear and soft under more normal conditions, was now blotchy and dry. Neither husband or wife, however, had red and puffy eyes, indicating excessive weeping. Perhaps they had done all the crying they could for their son years ago. They were wearing the same new clothes they'd had on for the funeral, but they wore them awkwardly. Lucille's words about none of the participants in the funeral acting as if they belonged there went through her mind.

The trio went into a coffee shop, decorated in the same bright orange as the lobby, and were seated at a small table near the window. From her seat Helen could see cars whizzing by on Hegenberger, speeding to the airport. "I'm sure you want to get to the bottom of this as quickly as possible," she said after a very brief statement of sympathy.

They said nothing, merely sat and watched with gentle patience. Helen began by asking where they were from.

"Modesto, originally," Howard James said. "Got me a little appliance shop out there. New and second-hand. Good stuff, too," he added, reaching inside his jacket for a card. Helen accepted it with thanks, deciding that letting him ramble for a bit might be the best approach.

"I can remember," he went on, chuckling, "I can remember Danny helping us out in the shop when he was just a youngun. Remember, Dot? How he used to hate having to sweep and dust and all that."

"Yes, Howard, I remember," his wife said, looking not at her husband but at Helen.

"He always wanted to do big things, you see," Mr. James explained. "Modesto's like a small town, and Danny was always going off to San Francisco. He wanted to be in the big city. He even skipped school sometimes, hitching rides out with strangers. I'd tan his hide for him but he never paid any mind. Right, Dot?" This time Mrs. James didn't bother to respond. She stared at Helen with an air of resignation. Perhaps she had spent too many years being a sounding board for her husband.

Helen asked, "When did he first leave home?"

"Let's see now — that would be when he was eighteen, damn near fifteen years ago. Yep, without so much as a by-your-leave." Howard took a sip of his hot tea, slurping a little. His hand shook as he placed the cup back on its saucer. Mrs. James looked at the drops as if she would like to blot them away with her paper napkin. "We got a couple of postcards from him, though, didn't we, Dot? Telling us all about his prospects. That's what he called them, prospects."

"Did he ever tell you exactly what he was doing?" Helen asked.

"Well, no, not exactly," he answered, faltering. "I think one time he did say he was in sales or something of that nature. Like father, like son, I said, when I read that. I knew I'd taught him all he knew in the shop at home. It must have helped him to get started, you know." He looked at Helen eagerly, pleading for affirmation.

"I'm sure it did, Mr. James."

"Here, here's a picture of Danny." Before she could say anything, Howard had reached into his pocket and drawn out a dog-eared black-and-white photograph. It must have been taken before he left home. The camera had caught the cruel, sneering mouth, the bored slouch. All it told Helen was that he had been handsome in the James Dean style and that he had been miserable.

"Tell me, when was the last time you heard from him?" Helen asked, handing the picture back.

He scratched the stubble on his chin and thought. "I suppose that would be Thanksgiving. Just a month ago. He called us that day, didn't he, Dot?" This time his wife nodded. "He wanted to know if we could get the spare room ready for him, 'cause he was thinking about coming home for Christmas. I said, well, no problem at all, son. Come anytime."

Here Mrs. James made a small movement and an even smaller noise that Helen heard, though Mr.

James kept on talking. "He said he might be moving away from California. His company wanted to send him down to Mexico for a few years, and he didn't know when he might see us again." His chest puffed out a little, and he sat straighter, proud to be telling someone about his son's accomplishments in the world of big business.

"That would have been nice, Mr. James."

"He said me and Dot could come to see him down there anytime, once he got settled," he said. "Told me he'd fix me up with a couple of them señoritas and we'd never say nothin' about it to Mother. Dot knows we was only kidding around, though," he added.

"And that's the last time you heard from him?"

He nodded, sighing with regret at what might have been. "The next thing we know this policeman come around to the house." His hands shook more violently now. "Said there was some kind of accident happened — 'Scuse me for just a minute." He climbed out of his chair, wiping his eyes as he headed for the door marked "Men."

Mrs. James watched him out of sight, then leaned over to Helen and whispered, "Don't you listen to that old fool. He doesn't know half the time what's going on right under his nose."

"What do you mean, Mrs. James?"

"I mean that son of ours was no good. Never was, ever. Many's the time I tried to whale the meanness out of him. His dad did, too, though he won't ever admit to it. No sir, he's got to go around always talking like they were the best friends in the world." She spat her words out with venom, hunched forward in her seat, with the repressed force of anger at years of covering for the men in her life.

"Were you and your husband aware of what kinds of things your son was doing out here?"

She snorted. "He knows as well as I do that the boy wasn't in business. He never wanted to work, just expected things handed to him on a silver platter. 'Boys will be boys,' Howard would say. Sure, he'd whip him, but then he'd brag about how wild and tough his son was."

"Did he ever talk about his life here at all? Who he knew, who he talked to?" She had to ask quickly. Mr. James might return any moment.

Mrs. James shook her head and made a noise like a laugh. "Are you kidding? He was up to no good, I could see that. Don't you believe a word my husband says about it. Daniel lied and stole since he could walk and talk, and he got killed for it." Her pinched face showed no grief, only a stern look of contempt.

"Did you talk to him yourself when he called on Thanksgiving?"

"It was me that answered, not Howard. He told me to get his room ready for him, that he'd be out for Christmas. Like I was supposed to be waiting for him all these years, just waiting for his visit."

Helen saw that Mr. James was approaching the table, composed and cheerful. She smiled at him, thinking about the proposed Christmas visit. Maybe Danny had seen the house in Modesto as a good place to stay for a while after the bank job, a refuge until the furor died down. Then on to Mexico. But for what?

"Did Danny mention a friend? Someone who'd be with him when he came out for Christmas?"

"Nope. Never said nothin' to me about it. Did he mention that to you, Dot?" She shook her head . "I guess he was just figuring on coming by himself."

There seemed little else to say. Whatever Danny James' plans had been, he'd revealed nothing about them to his parents. As Helen rose to go, thanking them once again for talking to her, Mr. James grabbed at her hand, his sweaty palm trembling against hers.

"I know you want to do what's right, miss," he said, his eyes filling with tears. "I know you'll help catch that horrible killer that's running around loose while our son is stone dead and cold in the ground. You will, won't you?"

Helen reassured him, her stomach tightening with nausea. "Of course, Mr. James. I'll certainly do everything I can."

But it wasn't enough for him. "Because I want my son's memory cleared," he went on, still clutching at her hand. "I want honor restored to his name."

Helen stopped any further eloquence by pulling her hand away, almost rudely. "I understand, Mr. James. Thanks again." She turned to go, but not before she saw the look of disgust bordering on hate that Mrs. James was giving her husband.

Helen drove back to Berkeley with her car windows rolled down, savoring the cold air hitting her face. When she got back to the office, the red message light on her answering machine was blinking. It was Marita, asking her to come to the Tacqueria by the Claremont.

Chapter 20

Andre made a hasty exit from the restaurant. He was furious and he didn't care who or what he ran into. "Bitch," he muttered, loud enough to be overheard by several startled passersby. "I should never have taken her in when dear old Daddy kicked her out." He stomped out into the street, never hearing the horns honking around him. Still high, he was too restless to go back to his apartment right now. As he pulled his jacket tighter against the cold wind that had risen, he felt a rustle inside one of the pockets. Andre grinned, his anger forgotten. The photographs, the ones Danny gave him. They'd slipped his mind while he was talking to Marita. Andre was positive it was the girl in the bank in that one picture. Same eyes, same hair. Not dressed the same, of course, but you could tell the kind of body she had under that red dress he'd seen her wearing today. A few people standing on the corner with him were staring, listening to him mutter to himself, but he didn't notice. Instead, he went back across the street and walked up the three blocks to Ashby and College, heading for the coffee shop across the street from Greater East Bay Bank.

He had to wait almost an hour before Lorie appeared. The sandwich and soda he'd ordered lay untasted before him on the formica-topped table. He'd had to order something to be able to take a booth, but he wanted to get a seat that enabled him to see people coming in and out of the bank. Marita returned about a half an hour after he'd left her. A few minutes later, he saw Lorie walk out the front door.

With a muffled exclamation he tossed a ten on the table and dashed out onto College Avenue. Yes, it was the same girl — same sullen face, same hips. Suddenly his excitement turned to dismay. Lorie stopped and turned around as if waiting for something. A moment later another woman came out of the bank. This was a short and heavy woman, with an unhappy face, whose limp brown hair kept blowing into her eyes. Lorie was waiting for this one, it seemed. "Come on, Mattie," Andre heard Lorie say. "We only have an hour."

"Oh, shit!" the other one exclaimed. She slapped

a hand dramatically to her forehead. "I forgot. I have to cash a check."

Lorie rolled her eyes and sighed. "Jesus Christ! Well, hurry up." Plain Jane hurried back inside.

Andre crossed the street, feeling nervous and jubilant at the same time. It was now or never. He'd probably never get another chance to talk to her. "Excuse me," he said, putting on his best smile.

Lorie glanced at him with surprised contempt, then looked away. "Get the fuck away from me, asshole," she said in a bored voice, looking out onto the street.

"Hey, that's no way to talk! You don't know how much you want to get to know me." He edged closer, putting his face near hers. God, she was really beautiful. Danny had good taste. Did have, at least.

He was making her nervous, he could tell. Closing in on people always made them uneasy. It was like they all had this invisible wall that they hated anyone to get around. Well, he was going to get around hers. Who knew, she might even like it. "If you don't get away from me," she said through gritted teeth, "I am calling a cop."

"Now that's not very nice."

"Nice? You're not being very nice to me right now." She finally looked at him directly. "Hey. Wait a minute. Weren't you in there just now?" She gestured back at the bank. Realization had dawned. "You're Marita's brother, aren't you?"

"In the flesh." He spread his arms open and bowed mockingly to her. "If you don't treat me nice I'll have to tell on you to my sister."

He'd figured her right. She couldn't resist male

159

attention, no matter who it was from. She began to soften a little, curious now. "So what do you want?"

"Well —" He began to steer her away from the bank. He took her arm. She didn't try to fight him off. "Let's just say I have something for sale."

Lorie laughed. "What? A car? Or something a little more interesting? Right out here on College Avenue?" She shook her head, amused. "You really are weird, more weird than your sister."

They were walking down Ashby. He looked for a good place to talk and spotted a cafe just ahead of them. The tables set up outside were empty because of the cold, although Andre could see that the inside of the cafe was filled with people. "Let's have a seat right here and talk for a bit, okay?" He was still holding her arm, and he guided her to one of the shaky stools, using more force than was necessary.

"Now I know you're crazy!" Lorie pouted. "Why do you want to sit outside? It's too cold. Let's get a table inside."

He stopped her with a look. "Outside is better."

"Hey listen, my friend Mattie is going to come looking for me," Lorie threatened. "You'd better not try anything."

"Will you shut your trap?" The five lines of coke he'd taken right before meeting Marita were still having an effect on him, and he was getting angry with her. Without any thought of who else might see, he drew the pictures out from his jacket and held them so that she could get a good look.

Her reaction couldn't have been more gratifying. Her lovely features seemed to withdraw and pinch themselves back into her face, the green eyes rounded with horror. Lorie made an instinctive grab for the

160

pictures, but he held them just out of reach, dangling them with malicious glee.

"My God! she cried, putting up a trembling hand to shield her face from view. "You asshole! Put them away, for God's sake."

Andre giggled, his good humor restored. "Looky but no touchy." Then he made a great show of hesitation, as if he were dealing with an unsure business prospect. "You're sure, now? You don't want another look? Here, this is my favorite," and he made as if to point out some feature on a sale item.

"Just put them away and tell me what the hell you want."

"Now, then, that's more like it." He leaned back, smiling. "I think we can work something out here."

* * * * *

Mattie stood outside the front door of the bank, trying to button the overcoat that was too tight for her. Where the hell did Lorie go? She wanted to hear more from Lorie about what had happened between Ed and Mr. Neely but they'd been cut short by a sudden stream of customers. Mattie wouldn't have consented to go out with Lorie for lunch unless she had a good reason. Now here she was, stood up, wasting her time. She shook her head in disgust and started down the street to find a sandwich.

Wait a minute — wasn't that Lorie sitting over there? It sure looked like her. Lorie had been wearing a red skirt just like that. She was with somebody, too. Leave it to Lorie, Mattie thought with a pang. If she's by herself for two seconds she'll pick up the first guy she sees.

161

In spite of herself, Mattie walked a little closer, wanting to see what was going on. The guy looked familiar. It couldn't be, but it was. That guy Marita was introducing as her brother. What the hell was he doing having lunch with Lorie?

Mattie kept approaching, feeling silly as she did so. This is really stupid, she told herself, but she kept going. When she reached the produce store next to the cafe, she slowed down, making sure she stayed close to the bins of potatoes so Marita would be less likely to see her. Mattie pretended to be inspecting a stack of onions while she strained to hear what they were saying.

Marita's brother was talking loudly in a teasing fashion, but she couldn't make out much. Something about "pictures" and a deal. Oh, my God, Mattie thought. Pictures of a deal? Then maybe Lorie was caught up in something wrong. Then she heard something else — Lorie saying a few words, speaking very softly. It was inaudible, but it was definitely Lorie's voice. A word came through. Mattie nearly knocked over the onions when she realized that Lorie had said "Danny." Holding herself very still, Mattie risked looking directly over the vegetables at the couple sitting at the table. But it was no good. They had gotten up and were walking past her back to College Avenue.

"Can I help you with something, lady?" It was the Vietnamese owner of the market. He was impatient today. There were quite a lot of people in the store, stocking up on fruit for Christmas.

"Yeah. I guess these oranges. And some bananas." He bagged and rang up her purchase. She took the sack, deciding to get out of there and see where they'd gone. It was too late, however. Mattie couldn't see them anywhere once she'd gotten out onto the street again.

As she stuffed her wallet back into her shoulder bag she saw something. It was a torn piece of cardboard. Mattie dug it out. Oh, yes, she remembered now. It was that business card Lorie had thrown away the night of the Chamber of Commerce party. Mattie fitted the two pieces back together and held them so that she could read the name again: Helen Black, Private Investigator. There was an address on it. Shattuck Avenue. It sounded like it must be near the campus, maybe that new brick highrise. Good thing I picked this up, Mattie told herself complacently. I just knew I might need it some day.

Chapter 21

After she left the restaurant Helen headed for Telegraph Avenue to make one final purchase for Frieda. The cash from Donna Forsythe's retainer weighed like a stone in her purse, thumping against her side with force. It still hurt her pride to have to admit she needed the money. Helen was always touchy this time of year anyway. The warm colored lights, corny carols, blinking decorations — they all touched wounds in her mind and her heart. She'd never confided, even to Frieda, how horrible her childhood Christmases had been. "We don't hold with such pagan celebrations," her father used to say, watching her cry as she talked about how all her other friends got presents. "Just a bunch of infidel papists," and sometimes he'd hit her one for good measure if she cried too much. Frieda sensed each year that Christmas was tough on Helen, but she didn't pry. As she climbed the steps up to her office around four o'clock that afternoon, Helen was grateful that the Danny James case was keeping her mind occupied and her emotions in check.

As soon as she got inside her office, Helen took out the small figurine she'd just bought and looked at it again. Frieda had been looking at it and talking about it for weeks. Tonight it would join the other gifts Helen had stashed on the top shelf of the hall closet. She set the statue down on her desk slowly, her satisfaction mingled with a growing uneasiness. What was it that troubled her about it? Then it hit her. Its reclining posture bore a resemblance to the pose Lorie had adopted for Danny's photographs.

Helen put the statue in its box and wondered again whether Marita had ever posed for Danny in his studio. The wet pleading eyes Marita had displayed during their first conversation swam up into her mind. Helen was still convinced the girl was lying about something. "So why did you fall for it at lunch this afternoon?" Helen asked herself sternly. She could recall every detail of their meeting at the Tacqueria — the way they verbally circled each other, approaching but never touching. Wasn't that how she, Helen, had conducted her entire life, though? Never losing distance between herself and others — friends, lovers, not even Frieda. Donna had spoken so possessively of Marita, with pride of ownership

165

gleaming in her face, as if she were a fine car or a choice parcel of land. With Donna and Marita, the chains of the relationship were solid and clearly defined, based on money and power. She and Frieda, however, were caught in much more nebulous bonds. That didn't make the bonds easier to deal with, just harder to grasp.

Lost in these thoughts, Helen was startled to hear a timid knock on the half-open door. The woman standing in the doorway was short and heavy-set, with mousy brown hair that kept falling into her eyes. She kept pulling at her coat, which was too tight for her, as if she were trying to hide herself in it.

"I'm Mattie Wilson," she said, taking one step inside the room.

"Yes, I remember meeting you the other night, at the Chamber of Commerce party." Helen regained her composure quickly and smiled reassuringly. "What can I do for you?"

But she didn't want to get to the point, not yet. Mattie stopped in the middle of the room, and peered around. "This is a nice office. It's a new building, isn't it?"

"Yes, only about a year old." Helen put a chair near her visitor. "Why don't you have a seat?"

Mattie sat down with a plop. She set her large purse on her lap and dug in it for a moment. Her plump hand came up out of the bag with a piece of paper. Helen could see that it was her own business card. "Lorie tore your card up the night of the party," she said. "I saw her throwing it away and got it out of the wastepaper basket." Mattie offered it to

166

Helen, who saw that it had been carefully pieced together and taped.

Helen handed it back to her. "What is it you want to talk about, Mattie?"

Mattie looked down, twisting the strap of her handbag. "I'm not even sure I should be doing this," she said. Helen waited, patiently. Mattie hadn't gone this far to turn back.

Finally Mattie sighed and slumped in the chair. "No, it's right. Somebody needs to know about this. Someone has to stop them." She looked up at Helen. "I think I know who killed Danny James."

"Who?"

"It was Lorie Harris."

Helen picked up a pen and began playing with it, fingering it with both hands, gauging Mattie from across the desk. The woman was dead serious. "Why do you think she killed him?"

"Because I heard her talking about it today."

Helen leaned forward. "Tell me about it."

The whole story came out. How Mattie had followed Lorie and Andre from the bank to the cafe. How she'd overheard them talking about "pictures" and "Danny." Mattie had felt so upset, she said, that she'd left work early, right after lunch, so she could talk to Helen about it. "I knew there must be something wrong when I saw them walking together. I told Lucille I felt sick, and she let me go home a few minutes ago."

"What do you think they were talking about, Mattie?"

"Well — I knew that Marita had gone out to lunch with her brother. Maybe they're all in on it

167

together. Whatever it is, I know that Lorie's no good. I think she should be stopped."

Helen said nothing. Of course it all fit in with Andre's ridiculous blackmail scheme. That's why he had made such pointed references to Lorie when talking to Marita in the restaurant today. Possibly Danny James had mentioned her name, or where she worked, in trying to persuade Andre to help him out. "You're sure this was Marita's brother?" she asked Mattie.

"I'm sure, all right," she answered. "I guess both Marita and her brother had to know something about it, didn't they? I mean," she went on, warming to her own theory, "Lorie was telling me earlier today about how even Mr. Neely was getting in trouble because of Marita. Ed Grant was really letting him have it for hiring the kind of people that go out with this Danny James guy."

"Let me ask you something, Mattie. Why didn't you go with all this information to the police?"

Mattie looked uncomfortable. She began to twist in the chair and kept her eyes on her shoes. "Well, I don't know — I mean, I think things are going on, but I don't want the police to arrest the wrong person." She looked up and Helen saw that her face was flushed. "Why should Lorie always get everything she wants?" Mattie burst out. "Men, looks, money, all of it. I'm sick to death of looking at her. She doesn't give a damn about anybody but herself. It's about time she had to answer for her behavior." Mattie was near tears.

Helen spoke to her very gently. "I tell you what, Mattie. Why don't you sleep on it tonight? Let's both sleep on it. If in the morning you still believe that what you overheard had something to do with the murder, come see me and we'll talk to the police. Fair enough?"

Mattie heaved a sigh. "Yeah, I guess you're right." She looked away ashamed. "Maybe I sound like a real bitch, but sometimes I just can't stand it. Being around her, I mean."

Helen nodded. "I understand." And she did — all those years of hearing how fat and ugly she was, prettier, thinner girls laughing at her, her own family's castigations. "You fat slob, why don't you lose some weight? You won't find anyone to marry you, looking like that," her mother used to say. The extra pounds had come off when she'd left Mississippi, just as she'd shed her accent and her awkwardness. The hurt remained, however, just like Mattie's hurt would stay with her. God only knew what kind of things she'd heard all her life for not looking like all the other kids.

"I guess I just needed to tell somebody. I hope you're not mad? I mean, I guess I thought you could tell me what I ought to do." Mattie suddenly looked very young and scared, huddled in the chair and struggling with her coat.

"Of course I don't mind, Mattie. We'll talk about it again tomorrow, like I said. Okay?"

Mattie seemed satisfied with that and gathered up her things to go. Helen showed her out with a smile and a pat on the back, then went to her desk to think.

Maybe Mattie was right. There was a good chance that Lorie knew more than she was telling. If she was close enough to Danny James to be in on the pornography operation, it was likely enough she'd seen or heard something relative to the bank job. And now Andre had to go and be a fool and stick his nose in where it didn't belong. He'd probably get himself killed at this rate. Helen was sure his scheme was a strictly hit-or-miss plan. He would simply bother everyone at the bank until he got a response. All the same, she might give Manny a call and suggest they keep an eye on him, ostensibly as a way to get to the real movers and shakers among the Oakland traders.

Helen's thoughts were interrupted by the faraway sound of the university clocktower ringing its bells. It was five o'clock, and just beginning to get dark. She took a flashlight from her desk and headed back down the steps for her car. The fog wouldn't be rolling in for a couple of hours yet. With all the employees gone, it would be a good time to poke around the bank and see what turned up.

Chapter 22

Andre's apartment building looked even worse in the early afternoon, when the light was brighter. The same dilapidated cars sat in the street. A group of kids were hanging around one of them, beating on it with fists and pipes. They were too absorbed in destruction to notice Helen as she went through the door and up the stairs. It was disturbingly quiet here today. Her footsteps echoed through the hall, ringing back from the walls with an eerie sound. From the street she could hear passing cars, many of them reverberating with the steady pulse of rap music. The overhead light in Andre's hall was not working, and Helen located his apartment from memory.

The door crept open an inch or two as she knocked. The only light in the room came from the wide-open window opposite the door. "Andre?" she called out in a quiet voice. "Are you here, Andre?" She ventured further into the room. It was bare and cold, just as she remembered it. Perhaps he wasn't home yet. She turned to go, but stopped with her hand on the door when she heard a noise coming from some inner room. It wasn't a groan, exactly, just a sort of low, blank noise, a sound emitted by someone barely conscious. With a sense of fear creeping over her, Helen went toward the noise.

Andre was lying on his bed. A lamp was lit on the table next to his head, circling his face in an aureole of yellow. Helen went quickly to the bed, afraid he was ill or injured. "Andre!" she said urgently, taking him by the shoulder. He turned to look at her, and she knew what had happened when she saw his eyes. The pupils, huge and black, made his whole face seem gentler. He smiled at her dully, only the vaguest of recognition registering her presence.

"What? What's the — Who?" He babbled at her, still with that smile on his face.

The syringe and needle were sitting on top of the dresser, against the wall. Whatever he had shot up, he'd used it all. There was nothing else on the dresser, besides some rubber tubing. Helen studied him closely. He was likely to be like this for several hours. She wondered if it was worth the effort to try to talk to him about Lorie and the photographs.

"Andre," she began, leaning down over him. His

eyes opened again. "Andre, where are the pictures? The pictures of the girl at the bank?"

He giggled a little. "Some bitch," he mumbled. "What the hell you want now?" He subsided into a stupor, breathing in shallow spurts.

Helen stood up, exasperated. She thought hard. The police would have collected all the negatives and pictures from Danny James' place long ago. If any other pictures of Lorie existed, it was too late to find those. But she had to stop Andre from doing this. Seeing him in this state, it was hard to believe that he knew anything much about the death of Danny James. He'd just seen an opportunity when the pictures fell into his hands, that was all. Could Lorie have known anything about the murder? Helen couldn't discount that possibility, but she wasn't about to let Andre use possible evidence for his own greedy and mindless purposes. She had to find them.

Helen felt as if she'd been sitting there on the bed for a long time, although only a few minutes had passed. She started by looking around the bedroom. As bare of furniture as the rest of the apartment, it contained only the bed, the little table and the dresser. Andre kept opening and closing his eyes as she worked her way around the room, watching but not saying anything, beyond caring what was happening. The closet was completely empty — no hangers, nothing on the shelf above, no shoes on the floor. His clothes, jammed in balled-up masses in the drawers and on the floor, revealed nothing. He laughed a little as she shut the final dresser drawer. "Nothin' in there, baby," he said. "Whyn't you come back over here?"

Fighting down disgust, she went back to the bed and, shoving him brutally aside, ran her hands slowly through the bedclothes and searched his pockets, only to turn up empty-handed. Helen rolled Andre back into the middle of the bed and went into the bathroom. It was in worse condition than the bedroom, buried under months of dirt and grime. Her efforts revealed only a sordid collection of spoons and needles, along with the more innocent toothpaste, razor and toothbrush.

It looked like she'd have to go through the whole apartment. Damn, she thought that realizing the time she was spending could have been spent at the bank. And it was getting darker and gloomier outside, she noticed. Getting down on her hands and knees, Helen peered under the bed, using the flashlight she'd grabbed from her shoulder bag. Except for layers of dust, the floor was bare. Steadying herself by holding firmly onto the mattress, Helen pulled herself off the floor. Andre moaned as she jostled the bed. Too bad, she thought. Helen was getting mad.

She turned the table over, holding the lamp with one hand. Nothing taped to the underside. Back to the dresser, this time pulling all the drawers out onto the floor. The flimsy particle board nearly fell apart in her hands and she left the drawers on the floor. Using her flashlight she examined the interior of the closet minutely, but she didn't see any sign of a secret hiding place. A walk around the small room, looking into corners and feeling the floor, only made her dirty and increased her anger. Finally she grabbed a chair from the dining room and stood on it in order to reach the overhead light. Nothing.

Helen stepped down and turned back to Andre. She'd have to move him off the bed so she could tear that apart. She set down the flashlight and, by grasping his slight body under the arms from behind, managed to heave him off the bed and prop him up in the chair she'd used to reach the light. The mattress was thin and took no effort to fling onto the floor. Andre gained consciousness and attempted to get up when she tossed the mattress, but he slumped back. Her efforts were rewarded this time. The cream-colored folder she remembered was neatly placed in the center of the mattress, stuck on its underside with several layers of masking tape. With a sigh of relief Helen ripped it off the fabric. She opened the flap, which was worn with use, and saw the pictures of Lorie, still intact. Thank God she had found them quickly. Andre was no professional blackmailer, she reassured herself as she replaced the photographs in their folder. She was sure this was all he had on Lorie.

But now, of course, there was the problem of what exactly to do with them. Everything in her life and her experience told her she must turn them over to the police. For some reason, though, she balked at the idea. It was evidence — but how important was it, really? The police already had ample evidence of Lorie's involvement with the pornography ring Danny had been running. Would one or two more nasty pictures make a difference? In her heart of hearts, she knew it might, since Lorie could have conceivably been his killer. Still, she hesitated at the thought of handing them over to Haskell. Helen didn't believe that Lorie was a murderer. In fact, ever since the conversation with Mattie a little while ago, an idea had been growing in her mind. All she needed was a little more time, maybe one more day, to prove her theory.

Helen tucked the folder into her shoulder bag and was almost at the door, ready to go, when Andre stumbled into the room. "It's the private eye," he said to himself. "What the fuck is it now?" His eyes were still enormous and black, but he was making an effort to pull himself together.

"Nothing," she said, her hand on the doorknob. She hesitated. Was there anything she could do for him? He hadn't taken enough to make him totally unconscious. Andre was no novice at this game. The bad part, the sickness and the pains and the cold, would all begin when he started to come out of it. There was nothing to do but wait. Resolutely she went out into the hall, feeling the old weight settle around her neck and shoulders. There was no getting away from it, she decided. Responsibility and guilt hovered nearby all the time, waiting for a chance to cast its spell over her. Taking the badge off hadn't helped that.

Once she got into her car, Helen rested her head against the seat. There was a great deal to decide, and decide quickly. As far as the photographs went, she'd already come to the conclusion that she was going to sit on them until tomorrow. That would give Mattie a chance to think about it as well. The problem of Andre would still have to be settled. Helen could think of several clinics where he could have gotten help, but she reminded herself that he'd gone that route before, and that he'd failed. Still, it would ease her conscience if she gave it a shot. For now, however, she had to get going. After a moment's

176

thought she took the folder out of her purse and placed it under the mat below her feet. There was not much daylight left, and she wanted to go back to the bank for another look around.

Chapter 23

Helen arrived at the bank just before four o'clock. The security guard was closing and locking the back door and the last customer was hurrying across the parking lot when she pulled her car up on Ashby. Going on a little further, she parked on the same side street she'd used the other night and walked the short block or so back to College Avenue. The scene was less charming in daylight. Everyone looked pinched and strained, as if holiday shopping was taking its toll at last. Helen realized with a shock that it was Thursday, the twenty-second. Christmas was only a couple of days away.

In the dull light of late afternoon, she was able to see the bank's surroundings more clearly. Through the big glass door she watched people scurrying back and forth across the lobby. The staff was finishing up, trying to get out in a hurry and beat the rush-hour traffic. Her first impression — that the bank had a quaint Victorian charm — was reaffirmed, but she could see that the air of antiquity was also a liability. The paint that had seemed mellowed that night now looked merely aged, even peeling in several spots. She could only guess at the state of the plumbing.

Helen walked past the building, thinking that she might take a look at the unfinished parking lot in the daylight. As she went through the bank's back lot, she saw a cluster of people grouped at the back door of the building. Lucille, Jerry Neely and Ed Grant were in conversation just outside the back door. The guard was waiting, key in hand, just inside the door to let them back in. Helen remained where she was. She was just close enough to hear them. She remembered Mattie's mention of a fight between the manager and the auditor. They both looked uncomfortable, and not just with the cold.

"Thanks for stopping by again, Ed," Jerry was saying, rubbing his plump pink hands together. "I hope that information helps."

"I'll need to run down to headquarters with this report. I don't see any reason why the remodeling

recommendations can't be put through right away."
Ed was going down the steps and heading for his car
as he spoke.

The amenities continued for a moment, and Helen
suddenly realized that Lucille was looking directly at
her. The two women stared at each other, neither one
revealing any acknowledgment of the other.

"See you back here at six for that drink," Jerry
called out, waving at Ed with forced cheerfulness as
the blue Cadillac pulled sedately out onto Ashby. He
and Lucille hurried back into the building, escaping
from the cold, and Helen wondered if Lucille would
mention her presence to Jerry. She thought not. But
it was pointless to stand there deliberating about it.
She might as well go ahead.

The construction workers were, of course, busily
crawling over the framework. There was no sign of
the old man, Ben, wandering about the place. The
sunlight, forcefully breaking through the fog, shone
brightly down on the workmen and their equipment.
The whole scene was ordinary and mundane, losing
its surreal quality in the light. Helen went down the
sidewalk, wincing a little at the sound of
jackhammers and staple guns. She was sure that if
there had been anything to find among the cement
chips and sawdust, the workers or the police would
have found it.

Still there was that small wooded area she'd seen
the other night, a patch of grass and trees that lay
between the new parking building and the residential
streets just above College Avenue. The police would
have been there, too, but she wanted to get a look at
it, curious how this miniature forest had managed to
escape development. The neighborhood was a wealthy

one, however. The residents there must have felt the need for a buffer zone between themselves and the business section a few yards away. They'd probably paid dearly for it, too, but the manicured lawns and the beautiful restorations of old houses told Helen they could afford it. Just the kind of place where Donna Forsythe would live, she thought, allowing herself a small burst of contempt, born of years of scraping and hardship.

The fences running behind the houses were high, so Helen felt little fear of being watched as she tramped down the slippery incline. She only wished she'd brought boots with her, for the ground was very damp, and there were quite a few patches of mud. Taking a circular course, she noted that the mud had been trampled extensively over the grass — probably traces of the police search. She smiled to herself, thinking of Lieutenant Haskell trying to keep the area secure and preserve as much evidence as possible.

Was it a likely place for bank robbers to gather? Helen thought not, except for the fact that it allowed easy access to the side streets of the neighborhood above. College Avenue itself was a main thoroughfare for both Berkeley and Oakland, and people passing by in the early hours of the morning, if they weren't drunk, might remember seeing a lone car parked near the bank. The same was true of Ashby, the cross street she now faced. Although these roads were patrolled, few people would be awake before dawn to make a complaint about a parked car, and Danny and his killer could have been reasonably certain of an easy getaway in the fog by going through this small-scale forest.

When she had gone as far as she could, seeing ahead of her a tall wooden fence, she turned and started back, skirting the construction site on her left, with the houses on her right. Straight ahead was Ashby, with its steady flow of vehicles making for the freeway muffled by the thick trees. The heavy branches overhead, almost black with moisture, kept the ground from getting much light, and Helen stepped carefully in the mud, sliding a bit. She could hear the talk of the men working on her left, ranging from comments on the progress of their efforts to curses for the cold. The constant stream of noise, combined with the thick cover of the trees, ensured her invisibility. There was a low wall here, and a group of large rocks rested against it. Looking down, she saw mud plastered onto the grass, caked and trodden down. Haskell again, she thought. It would be easy to step over the wall by standing on these stones.

With a sigh she sat down on one of them, the cold surface producing a mild shock. She rubbed her hands together and her thoughts wandered to Ben, huddled out here every night. She really ought to see about getting him into a shelter, if he would accept help from her. An image of two figures making their way through the trees in the darkness crept into her mind. They would climb over the low wall she was leaning on, then scuttle across the parking lot, crouching low. One of them must have made some noise or similar disturbance, rousing the security guard into action. Bob Scanlon would then have stuck his head out of the back door to have a look, and then the blow fell, crushing his skull. He had been a heavy man. It would have taken too much time to pull his dead weight further into the bank than just inside the door.

Helen moved, trying to adjust the rock she'd chosen for a seat to a more comfortable position. She heard a scraping metallic noise. Each time she moved the rock she heard it again. She got up and with some difficulty lifted the rock, exposing the soggy ground underneath.

The ring of keys hadn't had time to suffer much from their burial in the damp soil. They still glimmered in what light was able to get through the trees, and Helen eagerly brushed away the clumps of dirt that clung to them. The letters "GEBB" were embossed on a medal that hung on the key ring. Holding her discovery in her hand, she looked at the rocks again and saw for the first time that they were in some kind of formation. A cross? An "x"? She lifted one and examined the ground underneath. The impression it made in the mud overlaid the pattern of footprints made by the police. So it had been done very recently. The rocks were all heavy, too, hard to lift and move.

The jackhammers and earth-moving equipment, her own absorption in her find — these things prevented her from hearing footsteps coming up behind her. There was a sudden blinding pain that felt like a sharp clear light stabbing her eyes and her brain. Then she fell into thick darkness.

Chapter 24

When Helen opened her eyes again the sun had gone down. Fog was just beginning to rise from the ocean and seep into the hills above Ashby. Every time she blinked Helen felt a knife piercing her head. What the hell time was it? She managed to get to her feet but felt a wave of nausea when she lifted her head. The bank's lights were still on. She could see them filtered through the skeleton of the parking building, now deserted and eerie. Stumbling over gravel she found her way to the back door of the building, struggling to control herself.

The look on Lucille's face told Helen what she must look like. "My God," she breathed, propping the door open wide. "What on earth —"

"What's going on over there?" she heard from Mr. Neely. He joined them at the door and reached out to help Helen to a chair. Ed Grant looked on. He seemed to be standing very far away.

"We'd better call up somebody," Lucille said, picking up a telephone. "Police, the paramedics, something —" She gestured vaguely, hesitating before dialing.

"No, no, I'm all right. Please don't."

"But you really should —"

Helen began to feel almost angry at being hovered over. "It's nothing. Look, if you insist on calling somebody, you can call this number." She told Lucille Frieda's number. Fortunately she was at home; Helen heard her responses to Lucille's statements. Ed and Mr. Neely settled uneasily into chairs and watched her.

When Lucille had hung up, she asked, "What happened?"

"I don't know," Helen lied. "It was getting dark and I must have stumbled against something. That's all. Then I saw your lights on, so I came up here." Already her mind was clearing a little, and she was wondering where the keys might have gone. She hadn't had a chance to put them into her pocket before being struck down.

"Where were you?" Ed asked, leaning forward a little, a thatch of white hair falling forward. "In that parking building? You shouldn't have gone in."

Jerry cut him off. "Oh, for God's sake, the poor woman is hurt! Don't start in with a lecture now."

"Well, she still shouldn't have been poking around there. It isn't safe."

While they argued, Helen looked around the room. The vault door, in the corner to her right, was safely shut. Spread out on the table before her were files and computer printouts. The audit must be finished, she realized, recalling suddenly the brief end of conversation she'd overheard in the parking lot. The parking lot — where all three of them had been standing, possibly seeing her go off into the trees. Any one of them could have come back to find out what she'd been doing there.

So far Lucille had been silent. She kept staring at Helen, trying to make a decision about what to say. Finally she turned away and told them, "I can tell you. She was out looking around in the trees."

Helen closed her eyes. So much for building confidence.

"What are you talking about?"

"Back behind the parking building. Looking for clues, I guess. This woman is a private investigator."

The manager looked at her with renewed interest. "Are you checking us out?" He seemed almost happy at the idea, probably visions of Sherlock Holmes dancing in his head, replete with pipe and deerstalker cap. Helen decided not to talk. Lucille would do it all for her now.

"Must be that Danny James, huh?"

"Jerry, I don't think you should be talking about this," Ed said in a nervous voice, fidgeting a little.

But Jerry ignored him. "You know, I think I saw you here the other night. At the Chamber of Commerce thing."

Helen nodded, then was sorry as she felt the pain

186

coming back. She'd have to go to the hospital, just to make sure there was no concussion.

"Someone hired you to investigate? It was you, Ed, wasn't it?" Jerry was enjoying himself.

But Ed was horrified, visibly shrinking back at the thought. He addressed Helen.

"I'm sure you'll understand how I feel, Miss Black. This is highly irregular to let people into the bank after hours. In light of what's been going on here, perhaps we ought to tell the police about this." His smooth, reasonable tones contrasted with Jerry's enthusiasm.

"Well, I'd say that's entirely up to Miss Black, here," Jerry responded. "Frankly, I'd be glad to see her put one over on old Haskell and his crew and figure it out herself. He's been acting like he owns the place. Worse than the feds."

Ed crossed his arms and legs. His right foot danced in the air from impatience. "That may be, but I think we have a right to know what goes on around here, especially when a murder was committed on bank property less than a week ago."

Now Jerry was irritated. It must have been an old sore spot, this haggling over who was in charge of what. "That strip of land is not bank property, Ed. It belongs to the city of Berkeley, for your information. If people want to roam around there and get themselves whacked on the head all day that's their business."

Helen wasn't fooled by Jerry's apparent generosity as to her own motives. She'd worked around men long enough to know a battle for territorial rights when she saw one. She suspected that this argument had less to do with her presence there than with a desire by both men to stake out a claim. Lucille was sighing with exasperation, perhaps regretting her revelation.

"Jerry, Ed, please! This is not the time to be getting into it again." The two men looked at her as if she'd just landed from another planet. "I think we should just be a little more concerned about what happened to her." She looked back down at Helen. "Can you remember anything?"

"I was standing next to the wall, that low one next to the construction. It was muddy, and the sun was starting to go down. I guess I just slipped." She looked at each of them in turn: Lucille, serious; Jerry beaming boyishly; Ed worried. For a moment she felt a little afraid of them.

There was a knocking at the door. Frieda at last. After having rested for a few moments, Helen felt dizzy as she stood up. She let herself be led out, passive as a child, to Frieda's car. Frieda said very little, and Helen was grateful. She was fuzzily aware that they pulled up in front of Alta-Bates Hospital. The doctor didn't ask any questions. Apparently women being mysteriously knocked out were no surprise to him in downtown Berkeley. "I don't think it's serious," she heard him say as she shut her eyes against the bright lights. "Just get her home to bed."

She must have dozed off after that, for the next thing she knew Frieda was settling her on the bed. Helen tried to talk, but she was silenced with a touch of Frieda's hand.

"Don't worry about it now," she said. "We can talk about it tomorrow."

Still in a childlike mood, Helen allowed herself to be tucked in. Ordinarily she hated feeling helpless and obedient, but it didn't matter tonight. She only felt slight twinges of shame. "Sorry," she mumbled to Frieda.

"For what?"

"For dragging you out for this. I should have been more careful."

"Hey." Helen looked up. Frieda was leaning over her, her face barely visible in the soft light from the hall. "Just give up being so macho for once, okay? It's all right to let someone care for you sometimes." A quick kiss on the cheek and she moved away.

There followed strange dreams — fog-shrouded streets, Ben wandering in and out singing hymns in his cracked voice, Donna and Marita holding hands and leading her to a room where a bloody corpse lay. The head turned and leered at her, then she saw it was herself. When Helen woke up in a cold sweat, Frieda was lying next to her. Helen carefully turned over, snuggled close to her, and fell back asleep. This time there were no more dreams.

Chapter 25

The next morning Helen didn't wake up tunil ten. Frieda was careful and quiet. "Well, it was about nine o'clock when I finally got you into bed. We were at the hospital for a couple of hours. I can just imagine what would have happened if you'd been really hurt, I mean bleeding to death or something. Or if you'd really had a concussion. A two-hour wait is pretty terrible." They were sitting at the kitchen table, Frieda having a second cup of coffee, Helen eating toast and tea.

"What were you doing out there, anyway?" Frieda

tried to ask casually, but Helen could see she wouldn't be put off this time. So she told her a little bit. Not much, but enough.

"I just wanted to get a look around the back. They must have come in that way, through those trees."

"So who followed you in there?"

Helen shrugged. "I have no idea."

"Well, obviously there's something to be found back there. I mean, they wouldn't have gone in and knocked you out if not, right?" She got up with a deep sigh and started to clear the table. "I think we'd better call the police."

"Forget it, Frieda. I started this, and I'm going to finish it." They were both a little startled at the sharp edge in Helen's voice. Softly, she continued, "I don't think I'm in any great danger right now. Whoever it was last night — if they wanted to finish me off, they could have done it then and there."

"Will you at least be a little more careful? Not go off into the dark by yourself anymore?"

Helen was about to laugh off the melodramatic tone, then she saw that Frieda's eyes were filled with tears. "Well — I'll certainly let you know before I do."

Frieda tried to smile. "Guess I'd better get to the studio. There's a couple of people coming out from the city today. You know something?"

"What?"

"I enjoyed putting you in bed last night. You almost never let me take care of you. You should try it more often."

Helen didn't answer. The old fears rose in her, and Frieda saw it.

191

"Oh, well. Try to get some rest today. I'll be back this afternoon." They kissed, Frieda's mouth lingering on hers just long enough to suggest desire. "Will you be here?"

"Of course. Don't worry." As soon as Frieda had gone, Helen took her untasted tea to the sink and got rid of it. Then she started a fresh pot of coffee. She was drinking her first cup when the telephone rang.

It was Marita. "I'm calling for Donna as well as myself. She wanted you to know we'd be in Sausalito for Christmas, but we'd like to talk to you today before we drive up."

That's right. Tomorrow was Christmas Eve. "All right, that would be fine. Did you want to stop by the office?"

"Well, Donna's picking me up from work this afternoon and we'll be leaving right away. She was thinking we could meet at the little coffee shop across the street from the bank. I get out of work at noon today."

"That would be fine. See you then." As Helen hung up, she wondered if she was imagining the slight awkwardness in Marita's voice. The undercurrents of attraction between herself and the younger woman at lunch the other day had been real. Did Marita feel uncomfortable at the thought of seeing her again while having Donna in tow? Helen showered and dressed with a growing sense of irritation. For some reason, these two women were getting on her nerves. Was it the dishonesty she sensed in Marita? Donna's flaunting of her wealth? She stopped her thoughts when they began to make comparisons between them and herself and Frieda.

Helen was still walking and holding herself carefully when she arrived at the cafe on College Avenue. She had had to call a cab for the trip to the bank, since her car was still parked near Ashby. Her head ached, and she fought dizziness during the taxi ride. When she reached the cafe, she sat facing the front of the bank, ordered coffee, and waited. One by one, the employees of Greater East Bay Bank were trickling out the door and heading to the parking lot on the other side of the building. Mattie was first, her face bent down in the wind. Next came Evelyn, walking with a quick, light step, head held high. She called out to Mattie, who turned and waited for her. Together they disappeared around the corner. Janet followed, alone. She was hurrying, but without Evelyn's happier bearing. Helen remembered Marita telling her about Janet's husband being laid off. Then came Jerry Neely, his face revealing an excited anticipation of the holiday. Looking for all the world like some avatar of Christmas spirit, he waved a plump hand at a couple of passersby, probably customers. Seeing Jerry reminded her of Ed Grant. Helen wondered idly if he would make an appearance through the door, then remembered that the audit was over. He was probably in the bank's headquarters in Oakland.

Marita and Lucille came out last, Marita waiting while Lucille locked the front door with a large flat key like the one Helen had seen briefly yesterday. They stood together for a moment at the sidewalk, their heads together, with a conspiratorial look. When they parted, Helen saw Marita check for oncoming traffic, then step out into the street. But she stopped abruptly, looking to her left. Helen followed her gaze

193

and turned to see Donna Forsythe approaching Marita on the sidewalk. Judging from Marita's expression, the young woman saw this encounter as something to be gone through, an event to be faced with resignation. Helen greeted them with as much equanimity as she could muster when they sat down across from her.

Marita stared. "Are you all right?"

"Sure. Why?" Her face must be a little pale after the ordeal last night, Helen realized.

"Nothing, I guess."

Donna had hardly looked at Helen at all. She leaned back in the booth, her eyes constantly straying to Marita as she talked. Donna was in an expansive, generous mood today. "I just thought we ought to talk before the holidays started. Marita and I are going to be out of town for a while."

"Where are you going?"

"She's going to give notice at the bank and come away with me. My family has a little place up in Mendocino, out in the redwoods. We're going to stay there for a bit until this whole thing dies down."

"I see." Helen refused to even look at Marita, who was staring down at her hands, clasped demurely in her lap. "When will you be back?"

"Oh, I don't know, a few days after Christmas, I guess. I'll call as soon as I get back."

"The police have been talking to Andre again," Marita blurted out suddenly.

Donna rolled her eyes, smiling a little. "Don't worry, sweetheart! I told you, we'll talk to my lawyers for him the day after Christmas." She turned back to Helen. "It can wait until after Christmas.

194

We're planning a real old-fashioned one this time, tree and trimmings and turkey!"

Helen felt Marita's eyes on her, asking for something. Approval? I'm not her nanny, for Christ's sake, she thought angrily. She's a big girl now. She doesn't need anyone to watch out for her. Aloud she said, "That's great. It sounds like fun."

"How about you?" Donna asked. "Do you have family out here?" She could afford to be friendly and interested now, since Marita was safely by her side.

"No. My family is all in Mississippi."

"Funny. You don't have the accent."

"No." I shed that, Helen thought, with a lot of other things, when I came here — the accent, several extra pounds, maybe even openness to other people.

"You're not going back there, then?"

"I have a lover in Berkeley." Helen was uncomfortable talking about herself. Donna didn't really care, but Marita hung on every word. "I'm glad you called today, though," she went on. "I wanted to ask Marita about something. Do you know an old man named Ben? Hangs out in the streets around the bank?"

Marita was clearly surprised. "Sure. I mean, everybody around here knows Ben. Talks about God all the time, goes around quoting scriptures?"

"That's the one. Have you seen him today?"

Marita shook her head. "Not today, I haven't. Why?" It dawned on her. "Do you think he saw something that night?"

"It's possible. I think my best course of action right now would be to find him and talk to him."

"Well, I know the police already talked to him,

195

but I'm sure whatever he said didn't make any sense. It's usually just babbling, you know." She frowned into her cup.

Helen described how she met him before the Chamber of Commerce party. "It was a lot of nonsense on the surface. Still, I think he saw something. He sleeps behind the building in that construction site sometimes."

"Is that where you were yesterday? When you got hurt, I mean." Helen was irritated that Marita asked the question. Remembering Jerry's excitement, however, she realized it would have been quite an item at the bank this morning.

Donna, of course, was bewildered. "Helen was at the bank last night," Marita explained. "She hurt her head outside."

"Yes, I was lucky some people were there after hours last night," Helen broke in quickly.

"Did you find something out there?" Donna wanted to know.

It was better not to tell yet, Helen decided. "Nothing much."

"I see him once in a while, when I go out for lunch," Marita said. "I could let you know, maybe, next time I do. Maybe even keep him around until you could get there."

"You and your lunch dates," Donna laughed. "First Danny James, now Ben. Why don't you ever call me up for a date for lunch?"

Suddenly a bell went off in Helen's head. A small piece of the puzzle shifted into place, then another and another. Donna spoke twice before she heard.

"What? Oh, I'll probably find him in one of the

shelters tonight or tomorrow. It will be pretty cold to be at the site."

"I never thought about that," Marita said. "Those shelters must be sad places to be during Christmas. Especially for people with kids."

"At least he'll get a good meal there," Helen said.

"Surely he wouldn't be that hard to find?" Donna asked, amused. "I mean, all you have to do is show a little money to these people and they'll come running."

Neither Marita nor Helen wanted to comment after that, so Donna took a last sip from her cup and got up. "We'd better get started, sweetie. You know what the bridge is like before a holiday. I'll just bring the Jag around the front." She swept from the booth and Marita nodded, docile.

Helen broke the silence. "Are you really going to quit?"

Marita shrugged. "Maybe. It's a dead-end job, really. Besides, depending on what the police do, it might be safer to stay with Donna." She glanced up and her face darkened. "Don't look at me like that! What do you expect me to do, hang around until they pick me up?"

"Why should they do that, Marita? Unless you really do have a reason to be afraid?" Suddenly the truth hit Helen, hit her hard. "That's it, isn't it? There is some connection. The pictures. You did model for him, didn't you?"

It was no use denying, Marita saw. "Only once. It was all so stupid, really. Like Halloween, or something. Dressing up in these ridiculous outfits. Only once, I swear. I was practically starving." Her voice and her eyes were pleading again, the familiar winning look. "Can't you understand? I'd just die if Donna ever found out."

You mean you might lose your meal ticket. Then Helen dismissed the thought as mean and uncharitable. "Any lover worth the effort would understand, Marita."

"Lover?" Marita snorted. "You think she really loves me? I'm just her pet pony for the time being."

A horn sounded outside. It was Donna, looking into the cafe windows impatiently. "See? As long as she's in control, everything is all right." Marita slid out of the booth, dragging her purse and coat after her. "Merry Christmas, anyway," she called out as she left.

Helen picked up the bill the waitress put before her. Donna hadn't even made the polite gesture of picking up the tab. One would never know she could have thousands of dollars for the asking. At least she'd been too absorbed in Marita to notice that Helen had not come up yet with any real leads. Sooner or later, though, she would wake up from this rather Victorian sexual obsession and start demanding value for her money. And why shouldn't she? Helen asked herself.

As she took out her wallet and carefully stood up, holding her head very straight, she heard some kind of commotion near the front door. "I got money this time," she heard a thin, high voice whine. "See? A whole twenty-dollar bill! Looky."

"Now, Ben, you know I can't let you in here." It was Helen's waitress, talking softly to the old man. She kept glancing nervously over her shoulder. "Come on, now, Ben, why don't you save that twenty and

198

take this food with you?" Helen saw, as she got closer, that the waitress was pressing a take-out container on him, trying to get him to leave.

"If I can pay, I can sit inside, same as anyone else, can't I? Lemme in," and he tried to push her aside.

Helen stepped up behind the waitress. "Come on, Ben," she said, taking the container in one hand and the old man's thin arm with the other. "Why don't you and I go out to my car? I'll turn on the heater and we can talk." The waitress looked at her gratefully and hurried back inside. Ben was too hungry and cold to protest as they went together to Helen's car a couple of blocks away.

Chapter 26

Twenty minutes later Ben and Helen were sitting in Helen's car, Helen holding yet another cup of coffee in her hands, her companion gulping down huge bites of a sandwich. He hadn't seemed satisfied with the meal in the plastic box. "What would you really like, Ben?"

He'd considered for a moment, thinking hard. His eyes screwed up at memories. "A hot roast beef sandwich," he finally pronounced.

So they'd driven a few blocks back to Shattuck, to a deli Helen frequented. The owner, a small Jewish man, was just on the point of closing up and going home. When he saw Ben, though, he relented and kindly donated two sandwiches, potato chips and coffee. Helen waved back at him as he scurried down the street after he'd locked up, pulling his jacket tighter against the cold.

The car was warm and snug. The windows steamed from the coffee on the dashboard. Too close in here, she thought. She was getting a good whiff of Ben's clothes as he stirred in the seat. He was almost finished with his sandwich.

"How was that, Ben?"

She got a grin for an answer. He pulled his hand across his mouth and reached for the coffee. "They's always tryin' to get me to eat them tuna things at that restaurant. That waitress is sure a nice lady, though. A true Christian."

"Too bad she didn't let you stay in the restaurant, Ben. I mean, seeing that you had money this time."

He looked upwards. "The Lord will provide for his own. And he did, didn't he? You turned up, prompted by the spirit, didn't you?"

"Right. I sure did. I guess now you can save that twenty for something else?"

"Well, I was thinkin' — maybe some new clothes. I had these almost a year now." He looked down at himself. "I oughta go over to the Goodwill store."

"How did you get that money, Ben? Did someone give it to you?"

She had asked the question casually, but his response was surprising. He looked at her, his eyes big under the shaggy gray brows, holding a finger to his lips in a parody of a stage whisper. "Don't let no one hear you talk about that money, lady," he rasped at her. Helen shrank back a little from his breath. "Them's the gifts of the spirit."

A memory stirred. Something he had said the other night. "Gifts? When did you get these gifts?"

"The night I was tellin' you about. That night when we was visited by the angel of death." His eyes rolled heavenwards again and he clasped his hands. " 'Member how I tole you about the gifts of the spirit?"

"Yes, I remember. Is this what he gave you?"

"See, I wouldn't just tell anyone off the street, you know. You took me in and fed me, just like the good shepherd of the Bible, so I know you been washed in the blood of the lamb. Not everyone who calls him Lord will enter the kingdom of heaven. But you — you are one of the elect."

"Then you can tell me about the gifts?"

"Well —" He rubbed his chin, considering. "I reckon I can tell you about some of 'em, anyway." Nodding to himself, he reached inside his overcoat. Helen held her breath.

His hand emerged holding several bills. "See, the spirit knows when God's own children are in need. He threw me this gold and silver 'cause he wanted me to know." With reverent, shaking hands, Ben fanned out the bills.

Helen counted quickly. Ten bills. Ten twenties, to be exact. What was it Manny had said? Two hundred dollars missing from the cash shipment. The bag had been cut open and two hundred dollars were missing when they took inventory of the vault contents. Resisting the temptation to touch the bills — Ben would surely hate that — Helen leaned over to look

202

at them more closely. They appeared normal enough, except they were all tinged with some kind of brownish stain. She felt cold when she realized what that stain must be.

"Ben," she said carefully, "I wonder if you'd do something for me."

He glanced at her with suspicion, as if the excitement in her voice rang in his ears like a warning signal. "Depends what," he muttered.

"Well, seeing that I'm one of the elect — you said so yourself — I wonder if you'd let me trade you one of my twenties for one of yours."

He shook his head vigorously. "Don't nobody get them twenties, lady. The spirit entrusted them to me, see? I would be backslidin' if I was to let them out of my sight. Just you remember what happened to those who touched the tabernacle," he added darkly.

Helen agreed quickly, afraid he would open the car door and disappear. "Okay, okay. I just thought it would be all right, but I won't if you say so. What about the other gifts, Ben? Can you tell me about those?"

But he was getting impatient. "Don't you know nothin' about the Lord? Don't you know he clothes the cold and hungry and takes care of them? You ain't been readin' your scriptures, I can tell that."

"Maybe the Lord sent you here to show me these things, Ben," she said, casting about in her mind to her own past, trying to come up with some piece of fundamentalist wisdom left over from her youth spent in revival tents. "You said he clothes the naked, feeds the hungry. Were there clothes, Ben?"

"Maybe they was," he said, the grin returning. "What else?"

She thought hard for a moment. "The keys. The keys of the kingdom. That was one of the gifts, wasn't it?"

He cackled and slapped his knees. "See? Inspiration from the spirit. I seen you out there, struck down by the angel of death when you tried to mess with the keys. The Lord tole me to keep them against the day of his coming. See what you get when you mess around with God?"

"The angel of death again?"

"Now, don't start on me about the angel. Like I said, I saw no man nor no woman — the angel is a spirit."

"All right, Ben." No point in pushing that one just yet, if it was going to antagonize him. But the clothes were another issue. Perhaps he still had them with him, stuffed into his backpack?

"But he did give you a coat, didn't he? To cover your nakedness. Do you think I could see it?"

Ben started to pull out a thick black piece of fabric from his bag, then seemed to change his mind. "I don't know. You askin' too many questions. You startin' to sound like them cops that was out there that day. Never leave anybody alone, they don't. How come you're so nosy about it, anyway?"

Helen tried another tactic. "Okay, Ben. I guess the spirit didn't really give it to you, after all. If you really had that coat, you wouldn't be hiding it, would you? Like hiding a light under a bushel."

That did it. "Well, I guess you can look at it. But just remember he gave it to me to take care of." He pulled the coat out. Helen looked at it without touching it.

He hadn't pulled it out all the way, so she

couldn't tell for certain if it was cut for a man or a woman. The black fabric was thick and wooly, matching the description Manny had given her of the fibers found in the vault. It was stiff now, sticking out of Ben's hands awkwardly. Stiff with dirt and clay — and something else, possibly. The same substance that marked the money Ben showed her.

"That's enough, now," he said, stuffing it back inside the backpack.

"I tell you what, Ben," she said. "Why don't we get you a place to stay for tonight? So we can talk about the Lord some more?"

But his suspicions were roused. "Just like them hypocrites at the mission," he said spitefully. His hand was on the car door now. "You ain't one o' them, are you? 'Cause they always be preachin' at you afore you can eat anything. And they don't know their Bibles one bit, I can tell you that." He took his unfinished cup of coffee and opened the door. "I was wrong about you, I guess." He began to get out. The black coat, stubbornly poking out from the zipper on the bag, caught on the door, hooked by a sharp edge of metal. Helen got out, too, but Ben had managed to free the coat and shuffle away in the direction of Ashby.

"Hey, stupid! Who do you think you are?" Helen turned sharply at the remark. It had been shouted out by a heavy middle-aged man who had brought his car to a halt next to her. "You almost hit me with that car door! Stupid bitch, watch what you're doing!" He stuck his head back in the window and rolled it up with a fierce motion, cursing the fools that didn't know how to drive in Berkeley.

Helen had no time to waste on him. Already she'd

given Ben a head start. It was no good now. The streets were filling up with commuters on their way home, some trotting towards their cars, some shoving their way to the BART station across the street. Angry and disappointed, Helen got back in the car.

It wasn't until she'd reached her house that she saw it. Reaching around for her shoulder bag, she noticed a dim spot of color that contrasted with the pale blue interior upholstery. A jagged patch of red plaid cloth, a thin weave of cotton and wool, was stuck in the door of the passenger side. It felt wooly to the touch, much like the black coat. The lining, she told herself, it's a piece of the lining. Her fingers found a small spot that was stiff, almost cracking when pressure was applied. In the dim overhead light of the car, she could see that the spot was stained with something brownish.

Forgetting her aches and pains she ran inside to call Manny. Please be there, she murmured as she dialed the station. The clock on her kitchen wall said it was five p.m. Maybe her ex-partner was still working.

Her luck was holding. "Hell, yes, I'm still here," Manny said. "I'm finishing up some paperwork that has to be ready for the courtroom the day after Christmas. Susan's not too happy, but if I can get done tonight, I'll have two whole days free, and —"

Helen cut him off. "Listen, Manny, who's in the lab tonight?"

"I don't know. I think Carl. How come?"

Good. Carl owed her a few favors, too. "Manny, find out if Carl can run a blood test for me, would you?"

"Right now? But —"

206

"Just ask him, Manny, okay? Tell him it's me."

"All right, all right. Hold on a second." Helen heard the soft click as she was put on hold. If Carl would run a test, she could probably find out pretty quickly. He was a good man. Come on, Manny. She held the torn lining in her hand, rubbing one finger on it, when she felt something else. Turning the piece over she saw that there was a bit of paper stuck to it. What on earth —

Gently she pried it away. It was more like cardboard than paper, really. A ticket of some kind. Although the printing was small she could make out the words: "GOLDEN GATE CLEAN—"

Manny came back on the line. "Yep, Carl is in. He says he's pretty backed up tonight, though. What's up?"

Helen sighed. "Well, I think I'm going to stop by with something for him anyway. Maybe I can talk him into it."

"Suit yourself. Do I get to know what this is all about?"

"I'll stop by on my way to see Carl. I think I may have something solid on the Danny James case. By the way, is Haskell around?"

"He took off somewhere a couple of hours ago."

"Never mind, then. See you in about twenty minutes." She hung up and went to the bedroom. Yes, there was the case file on the little table by the bed. She took it back with her to the phone and dialed information.

"We're sorry," the recording said, "all operator lines are busy. Please hang up and try again." Damn! She'd forgotten what trying to call on the holidays could be like. After two more tries, she gave up in frustration. She was trying to locate the Golden Gate Cleaners advertised on the ticket, and she was certain now what city it was in. As she waited one more time to get through to an operator, her eyes went back down the list of names and addresses Manny had supplied a few days ago. She fixed on one name and address — the name that had been clicking in her mind for several hours. At the meeting with Donna and Marita she'd been sure she was right. She'd just needed the evidence to prove it. Now she had it, right there in her hand.

When the recording came on for the third time, she slammed the receiver down. Screw the phone, she thought. It wasn't that far away. She would drive over herself and check it out. She gazed down at the address, fixing it in her memory, along with a name: 5580 Westlake Drive, Moraga.

As she went to get her coat, her eyes were caught by the sight of Frieda's gifts wedged on the top shelf, still unwrapped. With a sinking feeling she recalled the conversation, no, almost argument, they'd had recently. The drive through the Caldecott Tunnel shouldn't take more than a few minutes, but the least Helen could do was leave Frieda a note. Or maybe call her at the studio.

In the end Helen did both. She managed to get through to Frieda's number on the first try, but was deflated to hear the answering machine. "Sweetheart, I'm on my way to Moraga. I think I've figured everything out. I shouldn't be gone more than a few minutes, so I'll be back in time to help get Christmas Eve dinner ready for tomorrow." Then after a pause, "I love you. See you in a bit."

Leaving the note displayed on the dining room

208

table, Helen hurried to her car with a lighter conscience. She carried only her shoulder bag. Helen didn't need to carry the list with the address she would be seeking. It was etched clearly in her mind, along with the name printed next to it.

Chapter 27

Helen realized, with a sinking feeling, that she had misjudged how bad the traffic would be. She was going to be late tonight, and Frieda would worry, in spite of the note. But she needed to get the scrap of cloth to the lab right away for testing. And she had to see for herself if she was right about the killer.

She was almost at the station now, and she got off the street and steered around the squat, ugly building she used to call home. The lab was housed in a smaller, three-storied granite block beyond the parking lot. Most of the forensics were farmed out these days, but Helen knew she could sneak in a blood test without causing too many raised eyebrows. Carl could manage it. He came down to meet her when she called from the front desk.

Carl tried to find out what was going on. "I have to have something to tell them, I mean, about why I spent time on this." He scratched his scalp under the sandy crew cut and leaned his big bony frame against the wall.

"Come on, Carl, no one's going to know unless you tell them."

"Well, I don't know."

"Remember when Lancaster was found by the Marina? Who stuck up for the lab results?"

"I know, I know. All right, I'll try to squeeze this one in tonight."

"I owe you, Carl. I won't forget."

"Merry Christmas to you, too."

She went on down the hall past the desk sergeant. Manny would be in the staff room, typing with two fingers and cursing the day he'd decided to sign up. She was tempted to go back and seek him out, to tell him what was going on, but she decided not to. Helen hoped to have the whole picture ready to present to him on Monday, the day after Christmas. And to Lieutenant Haskell, she added, grimly.

At least she'd remembered to let Frieda know what she was doing. Helen felt better for having taken the time to call. She pointed the car toward Highway 13, taking the long winding road to the Caldecott Tunnel, keeping it in low gear. Just as she'd suspected, there was quite a backup on Ashby. No Christmas spirit was evident in the honking, swearing, red-faced drivers crowding all around her. Once, when she'd first moved here, Helen had been terrified of the cars darting with careless abandon on the freeways. Fear had made her drive about ten miles below the speed limit, prompting those forced to wait for her to lean on their horns.

"Don't worry, honey," Aunt Josephine had said, clutching the armrest tight and shutting her eyes at the close calls. "It takes a little while to get adjusted. Now if you turn here — that's it — we can drive by the campus." Helen smiled at the memory. That had been at Christmas, too, that first venture over the Bay Bridge into Oakland and Berkeley. Poor Aunt Josephine!

Of course, places like Moraga, where Helen was headed, were considered out in the country in those days. Contra Costa County, which lay beyond the tunnels and east of Berkeley, was a haven for those whose dreams were tied up in suburbia. Helen knew it as a series of bedroom communities, not quite little boxes made out of ticky-tacky, but very nearly. Staunchly Republican, white, and family-centered, the county was growing into unbelievable proportions now. The Bay area was simply running out of room. One didn't need to look any further than right here, in the middle of the tunnel, for confirmation of that. The two narrow lanes that linked Berkeley to the rest of the East Bay were a long string of metal reaching out to the freeways. Helen forced herself to be patient as she waited to get out on the other side, going over some of the facts of the case as she crawled along.

It wasn't just Lucille of course, who had worked with Danny James all those years ago. Jerry Neely had been around then, as well as Ed Grant. Hadn't Lucille said something about its being just like the old days, when Danny showed up again? All of them together.

Her car finally broke free of the tunnels, and the road branched out into five lanes. It had taken her nearly twenty minutes to get through. She kept looking for the right exit as she thought hard. Damn! She should have taken that last one. Irritated, she took the next one and circled back, turning on her high beams to see through the gathering fog. She'd been here once or twice before. There should be a road right here that led into the small town of Moraga.

Her memory hadn't failed her. Pulling into a gas station on the corner, Helen took a look at the map of Contra Costa County she kept with the other maps in the glove compartment. Westlake Drive crossed the main road about three miles from where she was. But what about the cleaners? There was a public phone booth just in front of her, but the yellow pages had been torn away. Only the thick binding hung forlorn from its chain.

Helen saw an attendant, a kid of about eighteen, standing in a booth. She approached him and heard a heavy metal band thumping through the glass. "Excuse me," she said, almost shouting.

With a pained expression he turned down the music and listened to her question. "Yeah, it's the only cleaners in town. Just go up the road to Westlake Drive and turn left. Across the street from the grocery store."

"Thanks." She sped off, the only car in sight on that lonely stretch of road that reached up into the dark hills. The fog was thicker here, settling in for the night in big patches. Slowing down, she saw the sign she was looking for and made the turn. There it was — a painted window depicting the Golden Gate Bridge in red and yellow. Her headlights picked out rows of shirts and coats, a little unnerving to see, like a silent waiting battalion. The number of the shop was 5500.

Helen found the house a minute later. It was set back from the street, and perfectly landscaped. Tall evergreens dotted the front lawn and lined the driveway. There was no light shining on the front porch to guide her to the front door, but a bay window next to the driveway displayed a fully decked Christmas tree with winking colored lights. The curtains were wide open.

Helen saw all this from the driveway, sitting just at the entrance with her headlights off. She couldn't see any other cars, but she couldn't be sure if anyone was at home. After thinking it over, Helen backed the car out slowly and parked it a few yards further up Westlake Drive. Not sure if she would use it, she stuffed the flashlight into her coat pocket.

Once on the front lawn, she stood still. No sign of guard dogs. No sign of life from the house at all. Her eyes were getting used to the dark, and shapes were visible. Apparently it was built along tudor lines, with lots of heavy half-timbering and phony little turrets and eaves. Walking cautiously she went across the wet grass to the bay window. She knew this was reckless, even stupid. She would just look inside the window and then be gone.

It was the living room. Everything was spotlessly clean, down to the crystal candy dishes on the coffee table. The only thing out of place was the woman on the sofa. Helen felt a brief moment of terror. Was she dead? She lay so still. Then she saw the empty bottle of brandy on the golden carpet next to the sofa. The woman rolled over and one hand flew out and slapped against the bottle, pushing it further under the coffee table. Her lips moved a little, then she subsided again. Helen felt relieved and turned away.

She decided to risk looking at the back yard. For the first time since she'd left the force, Helen regretted not being able to get official sanction to go into the house and make a thorough search. Manny had been right — it was very different doing something like this on your own, without being able to call in a back-up or get a court order.

There was a low chain fence at the side of the house. Helen easily climbed over it and landed on a patch of gravel. Her shoes ground against it as she edged along the house. Instead of a yard, there was a small paved area that overlooked another yard. Helen stood still and let her eyes adjust. She didn't want to stumble over anything and rouse the woman in the house. She was right to wait. Not two feet in front of her was a large plastic garbage can. There was little else to see — no furniture, no evidence of a pet, no plants. These were people who presumably lived out their lives indoors, windows shut, drapes drawn. She glanced down idly at the garbage can as the moon shone through a break in the fog.

The dim light glimmered on something there. She moved closer, stepping carefully. It made a strange crackling sound when she touched it. Mystified, she pulled it out. When she held it up to the moonlight, she could see something embossed on the long sheath of plastic. It was the same yellow image of the Golden Gate Bridge she'd seen a few minutes ago on the window of the cleaners.

Helen quickly gathered it up and rolled it tight, stuffing it into her coat pocket. There was no way Haskell could ignore this. He'd have to listen to her now. As she was going back to the fence she heard a couple of cars go by, horns blaring, kids yelling out of windows. Well, why shouldn't they? It was almost Christmas, after all. Once they passed by, Helen was struck with how silent it was in the neighborhood. The owners of these homes were able to insulate themselves from the kinds of noises Helen was likely to hear in her own neighborhood in Berkeley. The homeless mentally ill probably didn't wander these streets, howling at their invisible demons.

She got back over the fence and landed on the thick grass. Looking back on it later, she knew she had sensed something, some kind of presence, over in the trees. It all happened too quickly, though. She had no time to prepare. She was thinking about stopping at the phone booth by the gas station to give Frieda a call when it happened.

The cold round circle that rested on her spine was the barrel of a gun. Helen froze, still half bent over, not daring to breathe. "I'm surprised at you, Miss Black," said the voice. "You ought to know better than to be wandering out at night by yourself."

Slowly she turned her head and saw Ed Grant looking down at her.

Chapter 28

For a few minutes they stood there in the cold dark. It felt like eternity to Helen. "Let's see what you put into your coat," he said, speaking through teeth gritted from tension and cold.

It was pointless to refuse. Helen pulled out the rolled-up plastic laundry bag and gave it to him. He didn't have to unroll it to know what it was. Without moving the gun from its position he stuffed it inside his own coat. "What the hell made you want to take that?" he asked. "It must be the coat," he went on, muttering to himself. "But how did you find it? I saw them putting in dirt in the place I threw it the very next day. It must be buried." He prodded her with the gun and her heart gave an involuntary leap. "Come on, I want some answers out of you. I know the police didn't find it, or they'd be here now, too."

Helen didn't answer his question directly. "There was a bit of the tag from the cleaners stuck in the lining." Whatever might happen to her tonight, she didn't want to implicate Ben. If he went after the old man, the police would never know. They would assume that Ben was just another victim of life on the streets. And if she kept talking, kept him interested, it might buy her a little time. "It wasn't too hard to figure it out from there. You were the only one with the right address." While she talked Helen quickly glanced around, looking for a way out. It was dark. If she could just get away from the gun, she might have a chance of getting away. But it was grazing her ribs, fixed to her side. The least move might give him the jitters and then it would be over. What about neighbors? The closest house was a hundred feet away. She could hear the noise of a party in early stages emanating from it. They wouldn't hear anything over the loud music and the laughter.

"Stop it," he spat out, as if reading the thoughts racing through her mind. "There's nothing you can do." He looked down for a moment, meditating, then said, "I have to get you out of here."

"You're not going to get away with it, Ed," she said, trying to sound calm and confident, although she was aware that her words were the standard last-minute protest of every suspense story. "They'll piece it together, just like I did. In fact," she

218

persisted, remembering Carl, "the lab is running tests on the stains right now."

"So? Why should they link that coat to me?" Although he spoke in hard cold tones, she could tell he was sweating it out. His face was damp in the faint light from the moon. The hand holding the gun trembled slightly. Helen grabbed at this realization like a drowning man at a rope. Use that fear, she told herself. Work on it, build it up.

"Come on, Ed," she responded, encouraged to goad him in the right direction. Pleading for her life would probably make it worse, give him even more of a sense of power. "You know enough to know how much forensic science can do. There'll be traces of that coat on carpets, in your car, even on your other clothes."

It was working, just a little. "But they have to know whose coat it is first, don't they?" He was asking, not telling.

"That won't be hard for them, Ed. Look, I know you didn't mean to do it." The gun had dislodged from her body. It wavered a few inches away, no longer pointed directly at her. She went on. "You went in there after the money at first, right? That was all."

But the moment of trust had disappeared. Perhaps she had been too patronizing, too confident of her own skills. The gun was back in her side, poking at her painfully.

"Shut up, you bitch," he hissed. "I did a little checking up on you. I know something about you. You're a lesbian, used to be a cop. Couldn't make it there, so you went and blew everything to get this cheap agency going." He laughed, a high-pitched, terrible sound, that strained through his clenched teeth. "You thought you were pretty tough, didn't you? Butch, I think they call it. A lame excuse for a man."

Helen said nothing. She stood very still while he prodded her. What about taking a chance with a struggle, while he was mouthing off like this? If only he'd gesture a bit with his hands, sweep the gun away from her guts —

"I figure I'd be doing society a favor getting rid of someone like you."

"Another body, Ed?" She couldn't keep herself from asking. "It'll be tougher and tougher to hide them all. Where are you going to stop?"

But he wasn't listening any more. She could almost hear the wheels turning in his mind. Helen's thoughts followed his, and she suddenly knew, with a cold jolt in her stomach, what he was thinking. The hills that divided Berkeley from Contra Costa County were heavily wooded in scattered areas, and largely deserted. People didn't wander around in them too often during the winter. They were soggy and dark, since very little sun filtered down through the fog and the trees. She could think of several good spots for hiding a corpse. It would only be a matter of an hour or two to dump a body in any one of them. She felt Ed's eyes studying her. She wasn't very tall, but her build was sturdy and compact. It wouldn't be easy, but he would manage.

"Come on. We're going. We'll take your car." Of course. He wouldn't want that to be anywhere near his house. What would he do with the car afterwards? Probably leave it somewhere far away from the body, keep things confused.

They were back on the front lawn now, Ed following her as she made her way along the line of evergreens. Helen was a little surprised at how quickly her thoughts were moving, how aware she was of her surroundings: the way the grass squished under her shoes, the scent of the trees in the cold air, the noise from the house next door. She could try to make a break for it when they reached the car. Ed would be distracted by the physical necessities of opening doors and getting into it. It would be her best chance.

"Ed? That you?"

They both whirled around, and Helen almost cried aloud at the sound of Mrs. Grant's voice. She stood in the doorway, leaning on the jamb, outlined against the yellow light coming from the hall. One hand mopped her face, as if clearing away some interior fog. "Whatcha doin' out there, Ed?"

"Nothing, dear," he called out feebly, his voice cracking a little. "Go back inside and get some rest."

"Well, you come on in too." She hugged herself, shivering. "Jesus, it's cold out there. Come on inside."

"I will, I will. You go back in now."

"Huh? Hey, who's that with you out there?" She peered out, stumbling a little on the step and reaching out one hand to steady herself. "You got you some bimbo, Ed?" Instead of being enraged, Gladys Grant seemed to find the idea amusing. "Yessir, that's my Ed, last o' the red hot lovers!"

"Now, Gladys, if you don't get back in you'll catch cold —"

"I doubt it. Too well pickled for that." She was going down the steps onto the lawn, making sure she trod firmly as she warily descended. "Lemme just see who the hell this person is."

Helen waited, watched. Ed kept turning his head to try to watch them both, but the gun remained leveled at Helen. "Don't try anything," he whispered.

"I don't know you from Adam," Mrs. Grant was saying as she approached them. Helen could already smell traces of brandy mixed with perfume permeating the clean air. Ed's wife pushed her way past her husband, not yet seeing the gun, and stuck her face up close to Helen's. The combination of booze and nerves and fear made Helen queasy, and she couldn't help turning her face away. Mrs. Grant's face stayed close. Her breath puffed out in malodorous little clouds. "Nope, never saw her before." She turned to her husband. "Where'd you pick her up? Santa leave her in your stocking, Ed?" She tittered at her own humor.

Ed gave it one more try, keeping the gun low. "Gladys, if you'll just get back in the house, I'll make sure our neighbor gets home safely. It was dark, she got a little confused in the fog. I was going to walk her back to her house."

"Hey, what's this?" She'd finally seen Ed's gun. "Another stocking stuffer?" She peered closer, leaning over a little, and realized what her husband was holding. "Jesus H. Christ! That's a gun! What the hell you doin' with that thing?"

"Oh, God," Ed moaned. "For God's sake, will you please get back in the house!"

This was it. "Mrs. Grant," Helen said, "please listen to me. Your husband is in trouble. I think you can see that. Please —"

But she kept clinging to Ed, trying to hold him, on the verge of wailing piteously. "Oh, Ed, what's happening? Who is she?"

Ed pushed her away from him. Her eyes filled with tears and she clutched her fist to her mouth. "Get away from me, Gladys!" he cried. He stood back from them both, still pointing the gun. "Just get away!"

"Ed, no, put it down." She moved closer to Helen. Ed backed up towards the house, edging closer and closer to the front door. As he went further into the light from the house, Helen could see that his eyes were wild, darting around, looking like a trapped fox waiting for the kill, desperate to get out.

"Mrs. Grant —" She made a step toward the other woman, a few feet away. It was not so much an entreaty, but more along the lines of a warning. Helen kept seeing an image of the body of Danny James, lying torn apart on the floor of the vault. "Please stay back here, with me," she whispered, putting as much urgency as she could into her voice. "You don't know what he's liable to do."

"What do you know about it?" Mrs. Grant shouted at her. "He's my husband. I've been living with it for twenty years, all this time, and you think I don't know what he's gonna do?" She flailed Helen's restraining hand away from her and made her unsteady way back up to the house.

It was over now, and Ed knew it. His face was streaming with tears, and he put up a hand to his face, surprised to find it wet. "Ed," Gladys whined, "Ed, honey, come to me. Come to Mama." She knelt down on the porch before him, ludicrous in her

223

drunkenness. "Come on and gimme that gun. You don't need that thing, now, do you?" She made a clumsy gesture at him, reaching for the weapon.

Suddenly he quivered like a taut wire and leaped up. "No!" he screamed. "Get away from me! Just leave me alone, woman!" Startled at his shout, Mrs. Grant fell forward in a clumsy heap, her hand making a grab for the gun. It was all so fast — the thud of her body hitting the porch, Ed's screams, the piercing explosion of the shot.

Helen flinched, shut her eyes in reflex for a second or two. The tableau that she saw upon opening them was lit by the Christmas tree inside the house. In the green and red winking lights she saw Ed standing over the body of his wife, splayed out on the porch like a doll tossed down by a careless child. The gun dangled from his hand, forgotten. His face was a smooth blank, lines and creases eradicated by shock. Helen felt frozen to the spot, unable to make a move to the couple huddled on the porch. She could hear the sound of people next door, emerging from the house. In the distance but coming closer was a car, going very fast. She turned around when she heard it in the driveway behind her. The tires ground on the gravel as it came to a jerking halt, and Manny leaped out. Behind him in the street Helen saw two black and whites, lights flashing and swirling. Manny glanced at her, then he ran up to the porch. Frieda's voice was the next thing she heard.

"Helen! My God, are you okay?" Suddenly she felt arms around her, warm and soft, tugging her away from the scene at the house. "I was so scared when you didn't call back, I called up Manny. When he heard you'd gone to Moraga he thought we'd better come out and see . . ."

"The message." Helen was beginning to think again. It was Manny who had supplied her with the addresses of the suspects in the first place. He'd put two and two together when Frieda told him what she'd said on the telephone.

"Is she — is she dead?" Frieda was trying not to look at the body.

Helen didn't answer. Instead she buried her face in the soft down of Frieda's coat. It yielded to the pressure, enveloping her in softness. She was too tired to fight, too tired to even think anymore. Helen gave up to Frieda's arms.

Chapter 29

Helen sat once again in the hallway outside Haskell's office. The last time she had been here was just over six months ago, when she'd gone through an exit interview. She remembered sitting rigid with defiance for some time, while Haskell kept her waiting, making her angry. What the hell does he think he's doing? she'd thought to herself. One last power play before I walk. All the reasons for leaving the force replayed in her mind that night, taking on visual shape: the endless paperwork that often impeded the success of an investigation; impotent fury when hours and hours of hard work resulted in cases thrown out of court over technicalities; the constant barrage of machismo that sneered at her for being a woman. Even more important, of course, was the need to do something with her life, the struggle to get as far away as possible from the awkward kid who'd grown up in a slum in Jackson, Mississippi. A professional, independent woman, that was all she'd ever wanted to be. Aunt Josephine had understood that. Haskell, however, had been quite a different story.

The session had not gone well, not least because Helen knew she was taking a tremendous risk. She enumerated her reasons for leaving calmly enough. Haskell had sat across from her in his big chair, a buddha-like gaze meeting hers. He'd never liked her, nor made any attempt to hide his feelings.

That was six months ago. Things were very different tonight. Or it must be nearly morning, now. She glanced down the hall and saw Anderson, the desk sergeant, bringing Ben another cup of coffee. They'd located him in St. Anthony's Shelter, on Martin Luther King Drive, eating soup. He'd finally divested himself of his padded livery, even allowing Manny, who somehow managed to hit it off with him, to go through the contents of his backpack. Helen knew that Anderson had seen stranger things. He quietly sat and filled out reports, nodding serenely now and then at Ben's monologues.

Helen's thoughts went back to Lieutenant Haskell. An hour ago she'd sat in his office again, this time to explain how she'd gotten the idea that Ed Grant was the murderer. The joking reference Donna had made to Marita's date with Danny James reminded her of something she'd heard before — something Mattie had said in her office. "Ed was really laying into Mr. Neely about hiring the kind of people who go out with drug dealers like Danny James." That's what Mattie had told her. But how could Ed have known about that? Unless he knew it from another source — none other than Danny James himself. Maybe Danny had bragged about it to Ed, flaunting Marita as just another member of his private harem. Even ragging him about his own wife, who had been described to Helen as an embarrassment, a hopeless alcoholic. Could such taunting have set him off, angered Ed enough to provoke murder?

"An auditor is actually in a perfect position to get away with something in a bank," she'd explained to Haskell. "Everyone is too worried about covering their own asses when an auditor's around to pay too much attention to what the auditor himself is doing. In fact, they'd probably avoid him like the plague."

"So he had free access to all the records in the vault?" Haskell asked.

"That's right," Helen had answered. "Ed Grant was always propriety personified, a symbol of good behavior. No one would ever have suspected anything if he took a little too long in the vault or went snooping through drawers. It was a great setup."

Suddenly the door opened, and Haskell stood there, filling up the doorway with his bulk. "Thought you might like to hear some of this, Helen," he rumbled at her. She got up and went into his office.

Manny sat in one of the chairs set against the wall. An officer she didn't know leaned his tall frame against a filing cabinet. He nodded at her in a friendly way. Haskell sat down at his desk, gesturing her to the other chair.

The lieutenant rewound the reel-to-reel that lurched on the desk like a dinosaur. "Let me just find the spot. I think it's right here," he was saying, peering down at the counter with its whirling numbers. One thick finger pushed the stop button, another pushed the play button, and they suddenly heard Ed Grant's voice.

"It was all so easy. Because I'm an auditor everyone accepts everything I do. I guess they're afraid their names might go in some report somewhere."

"So nobody saw you pick up the keys?" Helen didn't recognize the voice. Maybe it belonged to the tall man in the corner.

Ed laughed. "That was the easiest part. The woman, Evelyn, she's a complete idiot. She left her keys sitting out every day at least three or four times. She left them by her teller window when she went to lunch that day, so I just walked up and took them."

"What about the combination? How'd you manage that? It's kept locked up in a cabinet."

They could hear Ed sighing. "It's just like I told you. They're all afraid of me." The pride in his voice broke through the exhaustion. "Whatever I ask them, they do it. If I want to see something they fall all over themselves to get it." He chuckled. "I just told Lucille one day to open up the cabinet where the combination is kept. I wanted to take out their supply of savings bonds and check them against the supply report. While she was looking for the report, which I'd hidden earlier, I reached in and took out the envelope with the combination. Easiest thing in the world, with that stupid broad."

Here Haskell interrupted to speed up the tape. "It's all pretty much bullshit for a while here, while he's bragging about himself," he said. "Now he starts talking about the time clock," and he pushed the play button again.

"All right, all right. Well, as I said, the vault door was in bad shape, and I knew the timer was pretty worn down. I also knew they were due for a servicing before the end of the year. As soon as I was told the date the alarm people would be there, I realized that was the only day I could do what Danny wanted. Although how you found out about it I'll never know. That woman, I guess. The one who came to my house tonight." Haskell cleared his throat and the others looked away and shuffled their feet.

"What do you mean, what Danny wanted?" the other voice asked.

"You don't think it was my idea to steal that shipment, do you? That was all his. No, I never did things on such a vulgar scale, you see. My projects were all so much more — well, discreet, you might say."

"Sort of artistic, huh?" the lieutenant said.

Ed missed the sarcasm in Haskell's voice. "Yes, actually. If only Danny had left me alone, things would have gone on as before."

Haskell stopped the tape again. "Let me just move it forward a little. Here. Now he starts talking about how they've been doing this for years, Danny cooking up schemes and Ed falling in with them."

"But why?" Manny wanted to know.

"Listen." It started again. Ed's voice droned on.

". . . so I started taking those wire transfers ten years ago, and nobody was ever the wiser. I mean, nobody got hurt, did they? Just a few dollars here and there from international exchange, things like that. It wasn't until Danny arrived that anybody found out."

"Takes one to know one, Ed."

"Don't you dare put me in the same category with that — that bastard! I was never like him, never!"

"Calm down, Ed. Go on, he found out you were stealing. Then what?"

"Well, he had some grandiose idea of a big bank robbery, I guess. Instead of reporting me to Jerry or anyone else, he said we could make quite a team. All I had to do was set it up inside, then he'd take care of the rest. Actually I did all the work. He just got rid of things, exchanged them, through people he knew. Drug dealers and other criminals, I think." His haughty voice plainly said that he considered himself to be in a different class of people from those Danny had done business with.

"What did you take?"

"Bearer bonds, blank cashier's checks and bonds, bank forms that they wanted to make forgeries. Anything."

"Not too shabby, Ed. You hop all over the bay area, picking a little here, a little there, and nobody suspects a thing because you're an auditor."

"It was fine, until he got this idea about the cash shipment. As if we could get away with stealing eighty thousand dollars!" Ed snorted in contempt. "He found out about the shipment from Lorie. You know, the slut who was modeling for him."

"So you knew about that, too?"

"Yes, yes, of course, it was a kind of hobby for him." He spoke impatiently, eager to get back to his own story. "Anyway, every time I'd try to get him to stop, he'd threaten to tell the bank everything he knew about me. All those years, all those things I'd done. It was no use. I had to do it."

"There was a fight that night, wasn't there?"

There was a long silence, then a deep sigh. "Yes. Yes, there was a fight. I told him he didn't have to kill old Bob Scanlon. All he had to do was knock him out. But he hit him a second time, really hard. I could see he was dead." For the first time Ed spoke with some emotion. His voice shook and he paused.

"The worst thing," he finally continued, "was when he laughed at me. If only he hadn't done that!"

"What happened inside the vault?"

"You can't possibly understand. Seeing him there, throwing that money around, it just made me crazy. I was risking everything just so he could have more money in his pocket. When I tried to stop him he laughed at me. Said I was a shriveled-up prick. Those girls — the ones he had working for him —" Ed's voice began to shake again. "He'd tease me about them and then laugh at me for not joining in with him, using them. Nothing but a bunch of whores, all of them. Including Lorie. Then he started in about Gladys. I just — well, I just went crazy, I think. I tried to hit him, to get him to stop laughing. Then he was trying to hit me and the gun went off." The voice was almost fading away now. Lieutenant Haskell switched off the machine.

"You were right about what he did with the coat and shoes," he said to Helen. "They brought Ben in just when he was telling us about them. Ed fell all to pieces at that, crying about his wife."

Helen shuddered inwardly, remembering the scene on the doorstep of the Moraga house. Haskell knew she was upset, and he spoke gently. "There was nothing you could do, Helen. She was killed instantly. Right in the heart."

"Just like Danny James." She looked up again. "Ed must have been sure the coat and shoes were buried in the dirt and gravel at the construction site."

"As soon as he saw what he'd done, he started panicking, like he did tonight. He knew he had blood all over him, he could see that he'd stepped in it on the floor. So he tore off the coat and took off the shoes. Then when he got out of the vault, carrying the coat and shoes, he realized he still had James' gun. He just shoved it down behind the closest desk, which happened to belong to Marita Spicer. Then he took off out of the bank, almost running, he says, throwing the coat and shoes into what he thought was a mound of dirt at the construction site. He'd forgotten that the keys were in the pocket of the coat."

"And he had no idea that Ben was hiding out there, and had seen them go in," Helen said.

"Ed panicked again when he saw you snooping around in back of the bank."

"Was the money in the coat, too? The two hundred dollars?" she asked.

233

"Yes. Ed doesn't remember too clearly, but he thinks he must have grabbed the money away from Danny when they started arguing, telling him to keep quiet and do what he was there for."

"Well, he won't have to be worrying about coats and shoes for a long time, now," said Manny.

"What's he likely to get?" Helen wondered.

Haskell shook his head as he put the lid back on the tape recorder. "Who knows? Neither death was premeditated. It's up to the lawyers now. And we all know how they'd love to wheel and deal with something like this."

Manny and the other officer drifted off, leaving Helen alone with Haskell. She felt she ought to say something to him, something encouraging friendship, but she didn't quite know how to do it. At least she could thank him.

"I really appreciate being able to hear his confession," she heard herself say rather formally. "I know it wasn't quite kosher —"

"Well," Haskell said with a poker face, "as a very young officer used to tell me when she first got assigned here, rules are meant to be broken."

She smiled ruefully. "Was I that arrogant?"

"Sometimes." He looked up and she saw a hint of a grin playing around his mouth. "But I'm beginning to think we should have tried to keep you with us just a little bit longer."

It was the beginning of a truce. Helen felt tired and relieved as she went back down the hall, too numb to really know and feel that it was over. She noted absently that Ben had disappeared. Anderson was on the phone, but she didn't want to wait and ask him where the old man had gone. She'd find out later. No one spoke to her as she went outside into the cold early morning air. The thought that it was now Christmas Eve, and that Frieda was waiting at home for her, quickened her steps.

Chapter 30

Helen sat in her office under the picture of Aunt Josephine. It was the day after Christmas. Donna had called her from Sausalito early that morning.

"We'll be in town for a while today. Marita is going to pick up a few things. I thought we could talk things over. You know, settle everything."

Helen had agreed, mostly because she didn't quite know how to say no to the woman. How could she explain that she'd much rather stay at home, nestled with Frieda in bed, Boobella curled at their feet?

They'd been like children yesterday, playful and self-absorbed, shutting out the rest of the world. Helen had found it easy to be this way, surprisingly; it seemed as though the debacle of two nights ago had released something in her. Today she was forced to put on the invisible robe of official behavior with Donna, and she was irked by the necessity. This was a very important client. She resisted the temptation to ask if it could wait another day and agreed upon a time.

"So he confessed to everything?" Donna was asking. She seemed almost joyful, sitting lightly on the edge of the chair, her face lit with interest and excitement. Christmas with Marita had worked a change in her.

"Yes," Helen answered. "Apparently he and Danny James had been doing this for years. He was in no position to refuse when James suggested going after the cash shipment."

Donna shook her head. "The idiot," she said. "I guess he'll realize what a fool he was when he's been in jail for a while." She spoke with carelessness, offhand about the events of the past few days, now that her own happiness was secure.

Helen stared. "It's a question of a little more than foolishness, Donna," she finally said. Suddenly she'd felt emboldened to call her client by her first name. "The man killed his own wife. He has no life anymore, no hope of ever going back to a career, should he get out of prison."

Donna's own temper flared. "And that wasn't idiotic behavior? Look, don't expect me to feel any sympathy for the man. He made his own bed with all those years of lying and stealing. He deserves to be punished. Not to mention what he put me and Marita through over the last week or so."

Helen gave up. "I guess I'm still just upset over what happened the other night," she said.

"Of course. It must have been horrible." Donna softened a little. She could afford to be generous now. "I certainly hope that this will make up for it."

Helen controlled her expression carefully as she accepted the check, which included her fee and a hefty bonus.

Donna laughed. "Don't be too shocked," she said. "I'm used to paying well for what I get. You did what I asked you, and did it well. Nothing about Marita or myself got into the papers."

"Thank you." Helen carefully placed the check in a drawer of the desk. "I suppose you'll be going back to Sausalito now."

"Yes. Marita will give notice at the bank, quit that godawful drudgery. I suppose we'll have to do something about that brother of hers, too. He called yesterday. I'd told Marita not to give him the number, but she did. Then everything can go on as it did before."

The mention of Andre reminded Helen of the pictures of Lorie. They were safely shredded into small pieces, tucked away deep in the dumpster in back of the office building, safely buried under the garbage of several days. "There are many clinics and centers he could go to for help. If you like I could recommend something."

Donna had gotten up from her chair and was restlessly wandering around the office. "What? Oh, that's quite all right, I wouldn't want him in a clinic.

238

There are several places in Marin we could check out." Helen knew the kind she meant — drying out places for those who could afford to pay a small fortune.

Donna stopped by the window. "Finally!" She went back to the chair for her purse and coat. "I told Marita to meet me here and we'd get started back."

Helen stood up to see her off. "Have a good trip. Thanks for coming out today." She felt very awkward, as if she were some kind of hostess at a party, trying to take care of all her guests, even the most difficult.

Donna gave her a brief smile, but her thoughts were all for Marita. Helen waited until she heard the elevator doors clunk together, then she went to the window and watched, rather sheepishly, knowing she was being voyeuristic.

There was Donna's golden Jaguar, parked in front next to Shattuck. Donna emerged from the brick doorway and waited by the car, but where was Marita? Then Helen saw her, walking down Shattuck. They began to talk.

Helen kept waiting for them to get into the car and drive off in splendor, but the conversation went on for some minutes, even growing heated. Donna was gesturing with her big hands, more animated than Helen had ever seen her. Marita stood very still, answering in monosyllables, her thick black sweater bunching at the elbows as she stiffly folded her arms. What was going on?

Finally Marita hung her head down, turned and walked away very quickly, leaving her lover to stand awkwardly on the sidewalk, feet slightly apart, making her look ungainly. The rich leather bag slid from her thick shoulder stopping at the wrist and banging at her ankle unheeded. Donna didn't go to her car until a young man, wearing only a thin sports jacket and muffler, bumped into her as he walked by. For the second time in just over a week Helen watched the Jaguar edge into Shattuck, but today there was no traffic to navigate.

She stayed at the window for a while, trying to understand why she felt so disturbed, wondering what it all meant. Had Marita suddenly gotten an attack of wanderlust, brought on perhaps by a stifling holiday? Donna had spoken as if this kind of separation had happened before between them. Maybe their relationship was founded on bonds of mutual pain. Donna would create a sense of imprisonment, while Marita constantly sought escape in the only way she knew. Helen believed, in spite of what she had just seen, that it would go on, a cycle of hurting and loving, back and forth.

All right, all right, she told herself. Go ahead. Make comparisons. She and Frieda did the same thing — circling one another like beasts of prey, wary of attack and longing to make a gesture of trust. And didn't she get caught up in her own power games, being tough and unyielding all the time? We back off at the last minute, Helen thought, only to start it over again.

Helen leaned on the window sill, feeling the cold through her elbows where they met the glass. It seeped in through her arms and enveloped her. She made herself stay there, thinking. All the times she'd held herself back from Frieda, from all lovers — she knew no other way. The surrender implicit in love terrified her. She could blame her frightened and

240

angry childhood, her years as a cop with all its horror and cynicism — the fact remained, she was aloof, deliberately remote from feelings. She didn't know if she could ever feel safe enough to be different.

As she leaned on the window, her eyes were caught by movement in the street below. A woman was approaching the building, carrying a large square package. Frieda moved with purpose, as she always did, her thin face set in determination. She was someone with somewhere to go. Helen watched her wait for a couple of cars to go by. What on earth was it? The shape suggested a painting or drawing. She'd said something about a new one for the office, and Helen knew it was her way of trying to understand and accept what the agency meant to her. As Frieda disappeared under the eaves covering the building's entrance, Helen felt the power Frieda held over her. No other woman had been able to reach in so far, to evoke such fear and love from her before. If only she could get beyond her terror of intimacy and open up, trust simply. Would Frieda be patient with her? Wait it out long enough for Helen to learn to love?

She turned away from the cold window and went to meet Frieda. They would choose the perfect spot for the painting, hang it up, perhaps try one or two places. Then they would go home together. Helen opened the door eagerly when she heard Frieda's step.

A few of the publications of
THE NAIAD PRESS, INC.
P.O. Box 10543 • Tallahassee, Florida 32302
Phone (904) 539-5965
Mail orders welcome. Please include 15% postage.

VIRAGO by Karen Marie Christa Minns. 208 pp. Darsen has
chosen Ginny.   ISBN 0-941483-56-8 $8.95

WILDERNESS TREK by Dorothy Tell. 192 pp. Six women on
vacation learning "new" skills.   ISBN 0-941483-60-6   8.95

MURDER BY THE BOOK by Pat Welch. 256 pp. A Helen
Black Mystery. First in a series.   ISBN 0-941483-59-2   8.95

BERRIGAN by Vicki P. McConnell. 176 pp. Youthful Lesbian–
romantic, idealistic Berrigan.   ISBN 0-941483-55-X   8.95

LESBIANS IN GERMANY by Lillian Faderman & B. Eriksson.
128 pp. Fiction, poetry, essays.   ISBN 0-941483-62-2   8.95

THE BEVERLY MALIBU by Katherine V. Forrest. 288 pp. A
Kate Delafield Mystery. 3rd in a series.   ISBN 0-941483-47-9   16.95

THERE'S SOMETHING I'VE BEEN MEANING TO TELL
YOU Ed. by Loralee MacPike. 288 pp. Gay men and lesbians
coming out to their children.   ISBN 0-941483-44-4   9.95
                                         ISBN 0-941483-54-1   16.95

LIFTING BELLY by Gertrude Stein. Ed. by Rebecca Mark. 104
pp. Erotic poetry.   ISBN 0-941483-51-7   8.95
                                         ISBN 0-941483-53-3   14.95

ROSE PENSKI by Roz Perry. 192 pp. Adult lovers in a long-term
relationship.   ISBN 0-941483-37-1   8.95

AFTER THE FIRE by Jane Rule. 256 pp. Warm, human novel
by this incomparable author.   ISBN 0-941483-45-2   8.95

SUE SLATE, PRIVATE EYE by Lee Lynch. 176 pp. The gay
folk of Peacock Alley are *all* cats.   ISBN 0-941483-52-5   8.95

CHRIS by Randy Salem. 224 pp. Golden oldie. Handsome Chris
and her adventures.   ISBN 0-941483-42-8   8.95

THREE WOMEN by March Hastings. 232 pp. Golden oldie. A
triangle among wealthy sophisticates.   ISBN 0-941483-43-6   8.95

RICE AND BEANS by Valeria Taylor. 232 pp. Love and
romance on poverty row.   ISBN 0-941483-41-X   8.95

PLEASURES by Robbi Sommers. 204 pp. Unprecedented
eroticism.   ISBN 0-941483-49-5   8.95

EDGEWISE by Camarin Grae. 372 pp. Spellbinding
adventure.   ISBN 0-941483-19-3   9.95

FATAL REUNION by Claire McNab. 216 pp. 2nd Det. Inspec.
Carol Ashton mystery.   ISBN 0-941483-40-1   8.95

KEEP TO ME STRANGER by Sarah Aldridge. 372 pp. Romance set in a department store dynasty. ISBN 0-941483-38-X 9.95

HEARTSCAPE by Sue Gambill. 204 pp. American lesbian in Portugal. ISBN 0-941483-33-9 8.95

IN THE BLOOD by Lauren Wright Douglas. 252 pp. Lesbian science fiction adventure fantasy ISBN 0-941483-22-3 8.95

THE BEE'S KISS by Shirley Verel. 216 pp. Delicate, delicious romance. ISBN 0-941483-36-3 8.95

RAGING MOTHER MOUNTAIN by Pat Emmerson. 264 pp. Furosa Firechild's adventures in Wonderland. ISBN 0-941483-35-5 8.95

IN EVERY PORT by Karin Kallmaker. 228 pp. Jessica's sexy, adventuresome travels. ISBN 0-941483-37-7 8.95

OF LOVE AND GLORY by Evelyn Kennedy. 192 pp. Exciting WWII romance. ISBN 0-941483-32-0 8.95

CLICKING STONES by Nancy Tyler Glenn. 288 pp. Love transcending time. ISBN 0-941483-31-2 8.95

SURVIVING SISTERS by Gail Pass. 252 pp. Powerful love story. ISBN 0-941483-16-9 8.95

SOUTH OF THE LINE by Catherine Ennis. 216 pp. Civil War adventure. ISBN 0-941483-29-0 8.95

WOMAN PLUS WOMAN by Dolores Klaich. 300 pp. Supurb Lesbian overview. ISBN 0-941483-28-2 9.95

SLOW DANCING AT MISS POLLY'S by Sheila Ortiz Taylor. 96 pp. Lesbian Poetry ISBN 0-941483-30-4 7.95

DOUBLE DAUGHTER by Vicki P. McConnell. 216 pp. A Nyla Wade Mystery, third in the series. ISBN 0-941483-26-6 8.95

HEAVY GILT by Delores Klaich. 192 pp. Lesbian detective/ disappearing homophobes/upper class gay society.
ISBN 0-941483-25-8 8.95

THE FINER GRAIN by Denise Ohio. 216 pp. Brilliant young college lesbian novel. ISBN 0-941483-11-8 8.95

THE AMAZON TRAIL by Lee Lynch. 216 pp. Life, travel & lore of famous lesbian author. ISBN 0-941483-27-4 8.95

HIGH CONTRAST by Jessie Lattimore. 264 pp. Women of the Crystal Palace. ISBN 0-941483-17-7 8.95

OCTOBER OBSESSION by Meredith More. Josie's rich, secret Lesbian life. ISBN 0-941483-18-5 8.95

LESBIAN CROSSROADS by Ruth Baetz. 276 pp. Contemporary Lesbian lives. ISBN 0-941483-21-5 9.95

BEFORE STONEWALL: THE MAKING OF A GAY AND LESBIAN COMMUNITY by Andrea Weiss & Greta Schiller. 96 pp., 25 illus. ISBN 0-941483-20-7 7.95

WE WALK THE BACK OF THE TIGER by Patricia A. Murphy.
192 pp. Romantic Lesbian novel/beginning women's movement.
ISBN 0-941483-13-4   8.95

SUNDAY'S CHILD by Joyce Bright. 216 pp. Lesbian athletics, at
last the novel about sports.   ISBN 0-941483-12-6   8.95

OSTEN'S BAY by Zenobia N. Vole. 204 pp. Sizzling adventure
romance set on Bonaire.   ISBN 0-941483-15-0   8.95

LESSONS IN MURDER by Claire McNab. 216 pp. 1st Det. Inspec.
Carol Ashton mystery — erotic tension!.   ISBN 0-941483-14-2   8.95

YELLOWTHROAT by Penny Hayes. 240 pp. Margarita, bandit,
kidnaps Julia.   ISBN 0-941483-10-X   8.95

SAPPHISTRY: THE BOOK OF LESBIAN SEXUALITY by
Pat Califia. 3d edition, revised. 208 pp.   ISBN 0-941483-24-X   8.95

CHERISHED LOVE by Evelyn Kennedy. 192 pp. Erotic
Lesbian love story.   ISBN 0-941483-08-8   8.95

LAST SEPTEMBER by Helen R. Hull. 208 pp. Six stories & a
glorious novella.   ISBN 0-941483-09-6   8.95

THE SECRET IN THE BIRD by Camarin Grae. 312 pp. Striking,
psychological suspense novel.   ISBN 0-941483-05-3   8.95

TO THE LIGHTNING by Catherine Ennis. 208 pp. Romantic
Lesbian 'Robinson Crusoe' adventure.   ISBN 0-941483-06-1   8.95

THE OTHER SIDE OF VENUS by Shirley Verel. 224 pp.
Luminous, romantic love story.   ISBN 0-941483-07-X   8.95

DREAMS AND SWORDS by Katherine V. Forrest. 192 pp.
Romantic, erotic, imaginative stories.   ISBN 0-941483-03-7   8.95

MEMORY BOARD by Jane Rule. 336 pp. Memorable novel
about an aging Lesbian couple.   ISBN 0-941483-02-9   9.95

THE ALWAYS ANONYMOUS BEAST by Lauren Wright
Douglas. 224 pp. A Caitlin Reese mystery. First in a series.
ISBN 0-941483-04-5   8.95

SEARCHING FOR SPRING by Patricia A. Murphy. 224 pp.
Novel about the recovery of love.   ISBN 0-941483-00-2   8.95

DUSTY'S QUEEN OF HEARTS DINER by Lee Lynch. 240 pp.
Romantic blue-collar novel.   ISBN 0-941483-01-0   8.95

PARENTS MATTER by Ann Muller. 240 pp. Parents'
relationships with Lesbian daughters and gay sons.
ISBN 0-930044-91-6   9.95

THE PEARLS by Shelley Smith. 176 pp. Passion and fun in
the Caribbean sun.   ISBN 0-930044-93-2   7.95

MAGDALENA by Sarah Aldridge. 352 pp. Epic Lesbian novel
set on three continents.   ISBN 0-930044-99-1   8.95

THE BLACK AND WHITE OF IT by Ann Allen Shockley.
144 pp. Short stories.   ISBN 0-930044-96-7   7.95

SAY JESUS AND COME TO ME by Ann Allen Shockley. 288
pp. Contemporary romance.   ISBN 0-930044-98-3   8.95

LOVING HER by Ann Allen Shockley. 192 pp. Romantic love
story.   ISBN 0-930044-97-5   7.95

MURDER AT THE NIGHTWOOD BAR by Katherine V.
Forrest. 240 pp. A Kate Delafield mystery. Second in a series.
    ISBN 0-930044-92-4   8.95

ZOE'S BOOK by Gail Pass. 224 pp. Passionate, obsessive love
story.   ISBN 0-930044-95-9   7.95

WINGED DANCER by Camarin Grae. 228 pp. Erotic Lesbian
adventure story.   ISBN 0-930044-88-6   8.95

PAZ by Camarin Grae. 336 pp. Romantic Lesbian adventurer
with the power to change the world.   ISBN 0-930044-89-4   8.95

SOUL SNATCHER by Camarin Grae. 224 pp. A puzzle, an
adventure, a mystery — Lesbian romance.   ISBN 0-930044-90-8   8.95

THE LOVE OF GOOD WOMEN by Isabel Miller. 224 pp.
Long-awaited new novel by the author of the beloved *Patience
and Sarah*.   ISBN 0-930044-81-9   8.95

THE HOUSE AT PELHAM FALLS by Brenda Weathers. 240
pp. Suspenseful Lesbian ghost story.   ISBN 0-930044-79-7   7.95

HOME IN YOUR HANDS by Lee Lynch. 240 pp. More stories
from the author of *Old Dyke Tales*.   ISBN 0-930044-80-0   7.95

EACH HAND A MAP by Anita Skeen. 112 pp. Real-life poems
that touch us all.   ISBN 0-930044-82-7   6.95

SURPLUS by Sylvia Stevenson. 342 pp. A classic early Lesbian
novel.   ISBN 0-930044-78-9   7.95

PEMBROKE PARK by Michelle Martin. 256 pp. Derring-do
and daring romance in Regency England.   ISBN 0-930044-77-0   7.95

THE LONG TRAIL by Penny Hayes. 248 pp. Vivid adventures
of two women in love in the old west.   ISBN 0-930044-76-2   8.95

HORIZON OF THE HEART by Shelley Smith. 192 pp. Hot
romance in summertime New England.   ISBN 0-930044-75-4   7.95

AN EMERGENCE OF GREEN by Katherine V. Forrest. 288
pp. Powerful novel of sexual discovery.   ISBN 0-930044-69-X   8.95

THE LESBIAN PERIODICALS INDEX edited by Claire
Potter. 432 pp. Author & subject index.   ISBN 0-930044-74-6   29.95

DESERT OF THE HEART by Jane Rule. 224 pp. A classic;
basis for the movie *Desert Hearts*.   ISBN 0-930044-73-8   7.95

SPRING FORWARD/FALL BACK by Sheila Ortiz Taylor.
288 pp. Literary novel of timeless love.   ISBN 0-930044-70-3   7.95

FOR KEEPS by Elisabeth Nonas. 144 pp. Contemporary novel
about losing and finding love.   ISBN 0-930044-71-1   7.95

TORCHLIGHT TO VALHALLA by Gale Wilhelm. 128 pp.
Classic novel by a great Lesbian writer.   ISBN 0-930044-68-1   7.95

LESBIAN NUNS: BREAKING SILENCE edited by Rosemary
Curb and Nancy Manahan. 432 pp. Unprecedented autobiographies
of religious life.   ISBN 0-930044-62-2   9.95

THE SWASHBUCKLER by Lee Lynch. 288 pp. Colorful novel
set in Greenwich Village in the sixties.   ISBN 0-930044-66-5   8.95

MISFORTUNE'S FRIEND by Sarah Aldridge. 320 pp. Histori-
cal Lesbian novel set on two continents.   ISBN 0-930044-67-3   7.95

A STUDIO OF ONE'S OWN by Ann Stokes. Edited by
Dolores Klaich. 128 pp. Autobiography.   ISBN 0-930044-64-9   7.95

SEX VARIANT WOMEN IN LITERATURE by Jeannette
Howard Foster. 448 pp. Literary history.   ISBN 0-930044-65-7   8.95

A HOT-EYED MODERATE by Jane Rule. 252 pp. Hard-hitting
essays on gay life; writing; art.   ISBN 0-930044-57-6   7.95

INLAND PASSAGE AND OTHER STORIES by Jane Rule.
288 pp. Wide-ranging new collection.   ISBN 0-930044-56-8   7.95

WE TOO ARE DRIFTING by Gale Wilhelm. 128 pp. Timeless
Lesbian novel, a masterpiece.   ISBN 0-930044-61-4   6.95

AMATEUR CITY by Katherine V. Forrest. 224 pp. A Kate
Delafield mystery. First in a series.   ISBN 0-930044-55-X   7.95

THE SOPHIE HOROWITZ STORY by Sarah Schulman. 176
pp. Engaging novel of madcap intrigue.   ISBN 0-930044-54-1   7.95

THE BURNTON WIDOWS by Vickie P. McConnell. 272 pp. A
Nyla Wade mystery, second in the series.   ISBN 0-930044-52-5   7.95

OLD DYKE TALES by Lee Lynch. 224 pp. Extraordinary
stories of our diverse Lesbian lives.   ISBN 0-930044-51-7   8.95

DAUGHTERS OF A CORAL DAWN by Katherine V. Forrest.
240 pp. Novel set in a Lesbian new world.   ISBN 0-930044-50-9   7.95

THE PRICE OF SALT by Claire Morgan. 288 pp. A milestone
novel, a beloved classic.   ISBN 0-930044-49-5   8.95

AGAINST THE SEASON by Jane Rule. 224 pp. Luminous,
complex novel of interrelationships.   ISBN 0-930044-48-7   8.95

LOVERS IN THE PRESENT AFTERNOON by Kathleen
Fleming. 288 pp. A novel about recovery and growth.
                                       ISBN 0-930044-46-0   8.95

TOOTHPICK HOUSE by Lee Lynch. 264 pp. Love between
two Lesbians of different classes.   ISBN 0-930044-45-2   7.95

MADAME AURORA by Sarah Aldridge. 256 pp. Historical
novel featuring a charismatic "seer."   ISBN 0-930044-44-4   7.95

CURIOUS WINE by Katherine V. Forrest. 176 pp. Passionate
Lesbian love story, a best-seller. ISBN 0-930044-43-6   8.95

BLACK LESBIAN IN WHITE AMERICA by Anita Cornwell.
141 pp. Stories, essays, autobiography. ISBN 0-930044-41-X   7.50

CONTRACT WITH THE WORLD by Jane Rule. 340 pp.
Powerful, panoramic novel of gay life. ISBN 0-930044-28-2   9.95

MRS. PORTER'S LETTER by Vicki P. McConnell. 224 pp.
The first Nyla Wade mystery. ISBN 0-930044-29-0   7.95

TO THE CLEVELAND STATION by Carol Anne Douglas.
192 pp. Interracial Lesbian love story. ISBN 0-930044-27-4   6.95

THE NESTING PLACE by Sarah Aldridge. 224 pp. A
three-woman triangle—love conquers all! ISBN 0-930044-26-6   7.95

THIS IS NOT FOR YOU by Jane Rule. 284 pp. A letter to a
beloved is also an intricate novel. ISBN 0-930044-25-8   8.95

FAULTLINE by Sheila Ortiz Taylor. 140 pp. Warm, funny,
literate story of a startling family. ISBN 0-930044-24-X   6.95

THE LESBIAN IN LITERATURE by Barbara Grier. 3d ed.
Foreword by Maida Tilchen. 240 pp. Comprehensive bibliography.
Literary ratings; rare photos. ISBN 0-930044-23-1   7.95

ANNA'S COUNTRY by Elizabeth Lang. 208 pp. A woman
finds her Lesbian identity. ISBN 0-930044-19-3   6.95

PRISM by Valerie Taylor. 158 pp. A love affair between two
women in their sixties. ISBN 0-930044-18-5   6.95

BLACK LESBIANS: AN ANNOTATED BIBLIOGRAPHY
compiled by J. R. Roberts. Foreword by Barbara Smith. 112 pp.
Award-winning bibliography. ISBN 0-930044-21-5   5.95

THE MARQUISE AND THE NOVICE by Victoria Ramstetter.
108 pp. A Lesbian Gothic novel. ISBN 0-930044-16-9   6.95

OUTLANDER by Jane Rule. 207 pp. Short stories and essays
by one of our finest writers. ISBN 0-930044-17-7   8.95

ALL TRUE LOVERS by Sarah Aldridge. 292 pp. Romantic
novel set in the 1930s and 1940s. ISBN 0-930044-10-X   7.95

A WOMAN APPEARED TO ME by Renee Vivien. 65 pp. A
classic; translated by Jeannette H. Foster. ISBN 0-930044-06-1   5.00

CYTHEREA'S BREATH by Sarah Aldridge. 240 pp. Romantic
novel about women's entrance into medicine.
ISBN 0-930044-02-9   6.95

TOTTIE by Sarah Aldridge. 181 pp. Lesbian romance in the
turmoil of the sixties. ISBN 0-930044-01-0   6.95

THE LATECOMER by Sarah Aldridge. 107 pp. A delicate love
story. ISBN 0-930044-00-2   6.95

ODD GIRL OUT by Ann Bannon.	ISBN 0-930044-83-5	5.95
I AM A WOMAN by Ann Bannon.	ISBN 0-930044-84-3	5.95
WOMEN IN THE SHADOWS by Ann Bannon.		
	ISBN 0-930044-85-1	5.95
JOURNEY TO A WOMAN by Ann Bannon.		
	ISBN 0-930044-86-X	5.95
BEEBO BRINKER by Ann Bannon.	ISBN 0-930044-87-8	5.95

Legendary novels written in the fifties and sixties,
set in the gay mecca of Greenwich Village.

VOLUTE BOOKS

JOURNEY TO FULFILLMENT	Early classics by Valerie	3.95
A WORLD WITHOUT MEN	Taylor: The Erika Frohmann	3.95
RETURN TO LESBOS	series.	3.95

These are just a few of the many Naiad Press titles — we are the oldest and largest lesbian/feminist publishing company in the world. Please request a complete catalog. We offer personal service; we encourage and welcome direct mail orders from individuals who have limited access to bookstores carrying our publications.